THE
Ice Cream
CON

JIMMY DOCHERTY

Chicken House
SCHOLASTIC INC./New York

First published in the United Kingdom in 2008 by Chicken House,
2 Palmer Street, Frome, Somerset BA11 1DS.
www.doublecluck.com

Library of Congress Cataloging-in-Publication Data

Docherty, James, 1976–
The ice cream con / by Jimmy Docherty. – 1st American ed.
p. cm.
Summary: In Glasgow, Scotland, after getting mugged twice in ten
minutes, twelve-year-old Jake comes up with a plan to con the
criminals in his housing projects with the help of his closest friends,
until events start to snowball out of control.

ISBN-13: 978-0-545-02885-1
ISBN-10: 0-545-02885-X

[1. Bullies–Fiction. 2. Robbers and outlaws–Fiction.
3. Friendship–Fiction. 4. Glasgow (Scotland)–Fiction.
5. Scotland–Fiction.] I. Title.
PZ7.D66217Ic 2008
[Fic]–dc22

2007035321

10 9 8 7 6 5 4 3 2 1   08 09 10 11 12

Printed in the U.S.A.   23

First American edition, June 2008

The text type was set in ITC New Baskerville Roman.
The display type was set in ITC Franklin Gothic Demi Condensed.
Book design by Susan Schultz

"I did what I had to do."
—The Big Baresi

Dear Jake,

I hope this letter finds you both in good health.

It has taken me a long time to understand exactly what happened that day.

The truth is I'm still not sure I fully understand. I've gone over things a thousand times in my head, trying to work it all out, and just when I've ruled out the most ridiculous and far-fetched explanation in my mind, it keeps coming back to me, that it is the only possible rationalization.

You did it.

I still don't know how.

What I do know is that you saved my life, and I saved yours.

I owe you, and you owe me.

Remember that, Jake. I will come back to it later.

It was only a few weeks ago that my life changed forever, but it seems much longer.

That was when I first heard the name Baresi.

I wonder what it was that brought him to Lochrannoch Estates. Maybe one day you will tell me. . . .

CHAPTER 1

Nothing quite compares with the excruciating pain of being kicked in the goolies by a Caterpillar boot.

Jake rolled onto his side as the pain exploded from between his legs into the pit of his stomach. His hands clasped instinctively around his privates, but very, very lightly, because the thought of even thin air touching them made the pain worsen.

As he rolled on the ground in the cold concrete stairwell, gasping for a breath, he could hear the unmistakable cackle of Demi and Desiree Dubble.

He hadn't seen them coming, which was surprising considering the size of them.

"Ooh, is poor little Jakey Drakey having some trouble?" mocked Demi in her thick Glaswegian accent. It was her quite enormous leg that had dealt Jake the breath-stealing blow.

Jake couldn't answer; the pain had grappled up his neck and now held his tonsils in a headlock, allowing only the slightest high-pitched whimper to exit his mouth. The truth was he knew he wasn't just in trouble, he was in Dubble trouble.

"Hand over the money, Drake," sneered Desiree, "or this time Demi will take a running start before she boots you."

"It's all we've got," squeaked Jake. "You can't take it."

By now the pain had started to disappear, allowing Jake to rock onto his knees and crouch in front of the four Caterpillar boots that bulged with their owners' fleshy calves.

Demi lifted her right leg menacingly over Jake's head. "We can take what we like, Drake. Now, give us the dosh; we want to buy some chips."

The twin Dubble sisters were well-known locally. They'd left school two years earlier at the age of sixteen to start promising careers as muggers of kids. Their parents were very proud of their girls, and very often they would write to them from their prison cells and tell them so.

Jake winced as he crouched on his knees, his hands still clasped between his legs.

He might only have been a few weeks off his

thirteenth birthday but he was tall for his age. According to his gran, his height was something he got from his father. Yet kneeling in front of the Dubble Ds, his slender frame took on a more fragile appearance. His mousy brown hair fell over his hazel eyes as he raised his head to look at them. His red T-shirt bore white powdery clumps from the concrete floor he'd been rolling on.

"Our Demi gets really cranky when she's hungry, Jake, and she hasn't had a square meal since lunchtime," growled Desiree.

"I'm surprised she's lasted till two," groaned Jake. "Look at the poor girl, she's fading away."

Desiree glanced across at her sister Demi's portly belly and for a fleeting moment she looked puzzled. Sarcasm was obviously not something the twins encountered very often.

"Are you trying to be funny?" asked Desiree.

"No, no, no," replied Jake, the aching from his bruised boulders gently reminding him not to get too cocky. Something he was always in danger of doing.

"I've got an idea; you could call it a proposition."

"A proposition?" asked Demi.

"Yes, Demi, a proposition, a proposal, a plan, a suggestion . . ."

"What is it?" urged Desiree impatiently.

"Well, I haven't had a chance to think it all through, I've been a bit busy counting my goolies, but I think I might have a plan to get you your potato chips. Firstly, you don't take *my* money . . ."

Demi looked at him suspiciously. "OK then," she replied, "so how do we get the money for two fried catfish sandwiches, four potato fritters, a double hot dog on a bun, a bacon cheeseburger, two bags of sour cream and onion potato chips, and a bottle of Pepsi?"

"Diet Pepsi!" Desiree reminded her sibling.

"Aye, Diet Pepsi."

"Of course, it has to be Diet Pepsi," agreed Jake. "You have to think about your figures, girls. Take the 'c' out of chips and what do you have?"

"Quit stalling and get on with it," sneered Desiree as she paced in front of Jake. "What's the rest of your plan?"

"Well, that's the part I haven't thought of yet, but give me some time and I'll do a bit of business, see what I can flog, and get you some dough. What do you say?"

Demi raised an eyebrow at Jake before turning to her sister.

"I think we should go back to our own Aargh plan."

"What plan?" asked Jake.

Demi turned quickly, too fast for Jake to react, swung back her leg as far as she could, and with all her strength booted Jake right between the legs.

At that instant, something told Jake that his own proposal had been rejected.

"Aargh!" he screamed.

"Exactly." Desiree giggled. "The Aargh plan."

For a few seconds Jake felt nothing, as though even the pain had been caught by surprise. But it was only a moment's respite before the most excruciating aching he had ever felt in his life erupted from his privates and poured over him.

Now he couldn't even yell; his eyebrows suddenly shot skyward, as if they were being ejected from his forehead, and he merely peeped and fell forward.

"This is your last warning, Drake," yelled Demi angrily. "Hand over your money!"

Jake didn't even hear her, he was too busy tenderly checking that he had the right number of body parts in the right place.

"OK, there's one," he counted to himself as he fumbled. "Where's number two? . . . There it is! One and two . . . one and two . . . one and two and three . . . three?! Oh, thank God, that's my key ring in my pocket. All parts correct and accounted for."

Jake lifted himself slowly to his feet. When he

stood upright, he was tall enough to be eye to eye with Demi and Desiree. Now all that set them apart was the small matter of 316 pounds in weight.

"I can't give you the money," Jake groaned through the throbbing pain. "I need it to buy food for my grandma. It's all we've got to see us through the rest of the week."

"Money. Now!" Desiree demanded. Demi stepped back as though she was waiting for the go-ahead to unleash another of her Caterpillar crushers.

"OK, OK." Jake stopped her. "I'll give you the money."

Jake rummaged deep in his jeans pocket.

"I'll let your gran lick my chips bag," crowed Demi as she and Desiree jostled for position in front of Jake like pigs around a trough at feeding time. Jake did his best to ignore their laughs, but couldn't quite manage it as their bellowing cackles boomed down the stairwell.

"I'll bet you one thing, though," he muttered under his breath.

"What?" replied Desiree.

"You two must have a combined weight of four hundred, maybe four hundred and fifty pounds."

"So what?" said Demi, slavering at the mouth.

"I bet you put your belts on using a boomerang?"

At first the sheer impudence of Jake's question didn't register with the Dubbles, but slowly the realization crept in.

"You what?" asked Demi.

"Listen to me, Twin Tubs." Jake's tone changed from teasing to angry. "If you think for one second that I'm going to hand you a single penny from this pocket, then your brains must be as thick as your butts. If you want it, come and get it."

Jake vaulted the railing behind him and raced down the stairs. Immediately the Dubbles launched after him like chip-seeking missiles locked onto their target.

Jake could hear their heavy boots clumping down the stairs behind him as he descended two at a time. He was still hurting from the kicks, so the frantic running made him adopt an open-legged, openmouthed, ignore-the-pain technique.

The security door that didn't lock smashed open as Jake burst through the badly vandalized entrance to the apartments and raced across the cement courtyard.

He could still hear the Dubbles' pounding feet behind him, but unlike his stride, which had begun to slow, theirs seemed to be quickening.

Jake wondered whether someone had tied two

large pizzas to his back without him knowing.

He could feel them getting closer. He could see their shadows catching his as the bright sun shone down on them from behind. He could hear them slurping.

They're going to bite me! he thought, trying desperately to get some more speed from his legs. The corner of the block drew closer, and Jake prepared to make his hairpin turn. He glanced over his shoulder to see Demi and Desiree hot on his heels, showing no signs of faltering. He gritted his teeth, faced forward again, and sprinted round the corner. Then *BANG!*

It was like someone had extended the brick wall in that fleeting moment when he wasn't looking. But it wasn't bricks; it was a man's chest.

To describe what he felt the second his nose burst as pain would be a bit like saying that when his gran takes her pills she farts—it doesn't get close to explaining how much.

Jake fell back onto the ground, straight as a pole. The projects, the sky, and the two men standing over him spun around and around until he shook his head and refocused. "Get out of my way!" he shouted, wiping the blood from his top lip and trying to get up.

"Calm down, you're OK," replied one of the men. He was wearing a short black jacket and sporting a mustache. "Who are you running from?"

Jake didn't need to reply; the way the ground was shaking answered the man's question as the Dubble Ds rounded the corner behind him. Jake was sure that somewhere up on the eighteenth floor of this particular apartment building, a picture had just fallen off a wall.

"Oh, it's you two," said the other man, lifting his hands from the pockets of his long black overcoat and placing them on his hips. His hair was swept back and looked wet; it was only when you were up close to him that you'd realize it was bone-dry and brick hard.

Demi and Desiree stood over Jake in angry silence. Their breathing bordered on the violent.

"We saw him first, so the money's ours!" panted Desiree.

Jake tried his best to understand her last comment.

"Really, girls?" said the man in the overcoat. "Well, we think that this lad here shouldn't be giving you a single penny."

Jake looked up at Desiree and half-smiled — he didn't have the energy for a full one.

"His money belongs to us now."

Jake's half-smile froze on his face as confusion turned to realization and his safety turned to peril in a split second.

"What do you mean, my money belongs to you?" Jake asked tentatively as he edged away on his backside. The men didn't even look at him. Their icy gaze was fixed on Demi and Desiree, who by now had also started to reverse away from them.

"Trot along, ladies," snickered the man with the mustache before blowing them a kiss.

Desiree turned and walked away; Demi followed her, but couldn't resist bending down and slapping Jake across the head as she went.

"Now tell me, son," said the man with the rock-hard hair as he helped Jake to his feet, "exactly how much money are we talking about here?"

"It's all we've got, me and my grandmother."

"I'm no mathematician, lad, but that didn't sound like a number to me."

"It's only twenty quid, but it has to last us."

"Have you ever heard the saying, Look after the pennies and the—"

"—pounds will look after themselves!" Jake couldn't resist finishing the sentence.

"Good, son, you're sharp. Well, I have my own saying. Would you like to hear it?"

"Not really."

"You keep the pennies and give me your twenty pounds."

"I prefer the first one."

"And I would prefer not to dirty my shoes by kicking your scrawny little butt around the block. Hand it over."

Jake reeled backward as the other man grabbed him by the arm and started rummaging through his pockets. After first discovering two buttons, a set of keys, four fruit bubble gums, and a picture of a monkey in a wetsuit, he triumphantly pulled a twenty-pound note from Jake's pocket.

"It's been nice talking to you, kid," the man in the overcoat said sarcastically as they turned away from him.

Jake watched them walk calmly across the courtyard until he stood alone in the middle of the concrete maze of tenements. He wanted to cry but wouldn't let himself.

Get a grip, Jake, he thought. *You can't just start crying whenever you get mugged twice in ten minutes.*

It seemed like an age had passed by the time Jake dragged his feet around and headed back to his grandmother's apartment. Every step landed in a puddle of dejection as he splashed his way through the misery and headed home through the Lochrannoch Estates, its multitude of multistory buildings huddled in a circle, flanked on all sides by a mishmash expanse of smaller six-story walk-ups.

Jake sloped past a freshly burned-out wreck of a car; the nostril-widening stench of melted plastic mixed with water made him turn his face away until he was clear of it.

Just behind what remained of the boarded-up community center was Jake's tenement block.

Apartment 17a with its flaky red door was home to him and his grandmother. He could feel the blood still oozing from his top lip as he looked back across the courtyard.

"I'm not taking any more of this," he muttered angrily under his breath. "You'll pay for what you've done."

CHAPTER 2

"**Y**ou've got to go see Crazy Cortesi!"

At first Jake didn't reply, or show any signs of emotion. He just stared long and hard at his best friend, from whose mouth the words had tumbled.

"Aidan," he said eventually, "that's a great idea. Why don't you fetch yourself a cigar from the cellar?"

"We're three floors up, Jake. You don't have a cellar, just a sixty-foot drop," replied a bewildered Aidan.

"Exactly."

"Well, I'm only trying to help, mate. I don't see why you can't just let it go. You'll get some more money from somewhere."

Jake slid his back down his closet door until he hunched to a rest at the bottom. His bedroom was quite large compared with those of his friends. In the corner of the room he had an inflatable chair with the words *Max Power* emblazoned all over it, which he'd received free with his favorite car magazine. All around the walls were posters of Jake's favorite cars. Like the one with the blonde in rather short denim shorts carrying two spare tires, and the other one with the redhead covered in soapsuds as she washed the hood of another of his favorites, whatever it was called.

"So what are you going to do?" asked Aidan.

Aidan Murphy had been Jake's best friend since he was three years old and somehow managed to juggle the roles of his fiercest critic and fiercest protector quite well. He had short spiky blond hair and a penchant for lifting his top lip under his nose and sniffing loudly. Aidan would frequently find himself receiving attention from the girls in the housing complex, something which he neither understood nor encouraged.

It was he who had dragged Jake off Eddie Tierney that horrible day two years earlier, when the fists flew and three close friends became two.

Even if Eddie had deserved it, Aidan couldn't watch his two best friends trade blows when the insults ran out.

"Cortesi knows about every crime in these projects; he does most of it, so if you want to find out who those guys were, ask him."

The idea of walking into Franco Cortesi's garage and asking for his help made Jake's stomach fall out of the left leg of his tracksuit.

"That's a great idea. I'll just walk in and say, 'Hello, Mr. Psychopath, please don't kill me,' then the rest will be muffled on account of him standing on my face."

"So let it go then."

"I can't."

"Why not?"

"Because I'm like a dog with a bone."

"So go see Cortesi."

"I can't."

"Why not?"

"Because he's a big dog with a gun."

Pharrp.

The noise echoed down the hallway outside Jake's bedroom door.

"Here comes your grandma."

An uneasy silence fell over the room. Jake quickly stole a glance across the bedroom at Aidan, who was busy concentrating on anything except Gran's farting.

The bedroom door slowly slid open as Jake's grandmother edged her way inside with a tray of milk and cookies.

"We're nearly out of cookies, I'm afraid," she informed Aidan cheerily. "Jake went out yesterday to get some groceries and came home with nothing. Now he'll have to go back out again today."

Jake forced a halfhearted smile as he raised his eyebrows to his grandmother.

"So, what will you be doing today?" she asked them as she bent over to put the tray on Jake's bedside table.

Pharrp.

Aidan felt his mouth curl upward at the side but managed to stop it just in time.

"Don't know yet, Gran," Jake answered quickly, trying to smooth over the sound.

"Well, whatever you do . . ."

Pharrp.

". . . make sure you stay out of trouble. It's a dangerous place now, you know, full of hoodlums and hooligans and . . ."

Pharrp.

". . . unsavory types. It's a wonder none of you have been mugged yet."

Jake sighed and stared down at the large blue swirls on the carpet. He heard the door swish closed as his gran made her way back up the hallway to the living room, breaking *pharrp* wind *pharrp* with almost every *pharrp* step.

"She, um"—Jake cleared some embarrassment from his throat—"she's on pills for her blood pressure. She worries a lot, you see, about living in these projects. The pills give her . . . ahem . . . gas."

Aidan nodded his head in understanding; he wasn't hearing these words for the first time. In fact, anyone who had ever visited Jake in the past six years had heard this explanation, such was his grandmother's frequency of butt-trumpeting in front of guests.

"She doesn't go out at all now, you know."

"Yeah, you told me." Aidan sighed.

"She's too scared of being mugged. Ever since the accident, she's looked after me, there was nobody else who could. Now I'm looking after her."

"Let the mugging go, Jake," Aidan said quietly. "The last thing your grandma needs is for something to happen to you."

"I can hardly remember my mum and dad," Jake began slowly. "But sometimes somebody says something and it reminds me of my dad talking, or I see something that makes me remember what my mum looked like. And I don't mean like in a photo but in real life, how she looked when we were playing in the garden or something, do you know what I mean?"

"Yeah, I know what you mean," replied Aidan.

"Yesterday I stood watching those two plonkers who took my money, walking away, laughing and joking, and I don't know why but I just remembered my dad. I remembered one day playing on the swings and a bigger kid hitting me, so I went crying to him. I remember him saying, 'Jake, always stand up for yourself. Even if you think you can't win, you have to fight back. Or he's beaten you without beating you.' I remember it so clearly."

"So what are you going to do? How are you going to fight to get your money back?" asked Aidan.

"I don't know," Jake replied. "I don't even know who those men were. But you were right, Aidan."

"Was I?" Aidan wasn't too sure what he was right about.

"Cortesi is the one guy who will know, so it's obvious: I'll have to ask him."

Aidan shifted nervously on the bed.

"I know I suggested it, Jake, but to be honest, I wasn't being serious."

"I know." Jake smiled back at him. "But I am. I'm going to go see Franco Cortesi, our local homicidal maniac, because I'm the man of this house and this needs to get done."

"Bravo!" yelled Aidan triumphantly. "And what color flowers would you like on your coffin?"

"Red and yellow," replied Jake indignantly. "I'm going to need some help, though. Do you think Harvey and Sofia will help me think of what to say?"

"Of course they will," replied Aidan.

"Will you go down with me to Cortesi's garage?"

"Of course I will!"

"And will you come in with me to see him?"

A tense silence filled the bedroom.

CHAPTER 3

A cold wind whipped through the streets of Lee Avenue in Glasgow. It added to the gloom that hung in the air around the huge gray walls and the enormous steel gates. Wives were joined by parents and friends in a despondent single-file line, as one by one they waited their turn to troop through the small front door and visit their loved one on the other side.

Nobody in the queue wanted to walk through the door of H. M. Barlinnie Prison, even for a short visit, but at least *they* got to walk back out again.

A loud clang of metal sounded out across the vast concourse as a heavy barrel dead bolt slowly slid backward, clanging to a stop. Farther along from the main entrance a thin door was pushed open, and a very large man with a shaved head squeezed his way into the daylight. His own frame easily dwarfed the door frame he had somehow just managed to cram through, and he stood surveying the street and the entrance for a familiar face. There was none.

"See you soon, Scullen," barked a deep voice from the darkness behind him. The door swung closed with a dense metal thud, and the bolt quickly shot back into its lock. "Probably," muttered the man under his breath.

Out past the concourse on the single-lane road a black cab sat with its engine running. The driver folded his paper and placed it to the side as the now ex-convict walked toward him, clutching a see-through plastic bag with pretty much all of his belongings inside. The waistband of his blue jeans strained to hold the extra weight as his stomach hung over it. His denim jacket, which fit him the day he entered the prison, now clung tightly around his shoulders and arms. Seven years of little exercise had taken their toll.

The door opened and the cab rocked from side to side as the man heaved his bulky frame into the backseat.

"Where to?" asked the driver, glancing into his rearview mirror.

"The Lochrannoch Estates, please." The ex-con's voice somehow contradicted his appearance, being both soft and well-spoken.

The taxi spun around in a tight half circle and headed back down the road away from the prison gate. The man watched quietly through the rear window as eventually it dropped out of sight behind them.

"Do you live at Lochrannoch, then?" asked the driver, trying his best to make small chat.

His passenger's eyes stared back at him in the mirror.

"No, I won't be there long," the man replied. "Just a little unfinished business."

CHAPTER 4

Jake felt his stomach tighten and roll like a clothes dryer as fear and nerves spun his belly to within an inch of projectile barfing.

Timidly he looked back over his shoulder toward his three friends farther up the road. They had chosen the top of the hill as an ideal spot to stop at for two reasons. Firstly, it gave them an excellent view of Cortesi's garage at the bottom, and secondly, it was nowhere near it.

"I can't believe he's going to go in there," Aidan muttered through a fixed smile, waving Jake on.

"Wasn't this your idea, Aidan?" replied Sofia, her lips hardly moving.

"Yes, but I didn't think he would do it. Jake is really smart, normally."

Sofia Zammett was Jake's only friend who wore a brassiere. She had dark brown hair that curled around her shoulders and dropped halfway down her back. Jake thought that her eyes were the nicest he'd ever seen, even if he'd never noticed the color. He liked to look at Sofia when she didn't know he was looking. Usually she was too busy watching Aidan.

"Sometimes you can only push a dude so far before he snaps," said Harvey prophetically.

Harvey Albright had a habit of saying "dude." He had picked it up watching Hollywood films about dudes, and now everyone was a dude to Harvey, including his mum.

"Jake doesn't know what it is to feel scared," he continued, rubbing his head. Harvey had grown tired of his friends' constant gibes about the huge curly ball of fluff that masqueraded as his hair, so twice weekly Harvey ran an electric razor over his head to keep his 'fro at bay.

"Do you honestly think Jake won't be feeling just a wee bit frightened?" Sofia questioned Harvey with a furrowed brow.

Harvey looked down the hill to Jake, who was almost at the entrance to Cortesi's garage. "Nah, you're right," he replied. "Jake's bricking himself."

Play it cool, Jakey boy, play it cool, Jake thought to himself as his legs dragged him closer to the garage. *Don't let them know you're bricking yourself.*

The hammering of metal and the clicking of ratchets became louder the closer he got. Steel-roller shutters hung halfway down the two large garage doors like lazy eyelids. Up above them hung the sign CORTESI AUTOS in green, white, and red colors to match the Italian flag.

As he reached the entrance to the garage, Jake paused for a second to collect his thoughts. Except he didn't just want to collect them, he wanted to pick through them and choose the one that told him to book back up the hill to his friends.

What's the worst he can do to you? Jake asked himself. *Actually I know the answer to that, but he would need a welding torch, some barbed wire, and a pair of pliers . . . all of which he probably has.*

The inside of the garage was very dark. Jake stood in the center of the first doorway and peered inside. He couldn't see anyone. The only indication he had that people were there was the symphony of drilling, hammering, and welding sparks.

"Hello!" Jake tried to shout but his tongue lassoed the words and yanked them back into his mouth. He tried again, "Is there anybody there?" He took a few steps inside the garage. The musty stench of motor oil and gasoline was everywhere. Slowly Jake's eyes adapted to his darker surroundings and focused on a few men working on some cars in the right-hand bay; none of them appeared to hear him.

"Excuse me!" Jake yelled loud enough to be heard over the small transistor radio blaring away in the corner. "I need to see Mr. Cortesi."

The clanging of a metal wrench hitting the concrete floor made Jake jolt; one of the men threw down his tool and turned toward him.

"What do you want with him?" he growled back at Jake.

"I need to see him about a mugging that happened yesterday."

"Are you dropping off his cut?"

"Yes, I am." Jake thought this was the answer most likely to get him an audience with Crazy Cortesi. Sure enough, the man pointed him to a door at the far side of the garage.

Jake made his way through the oily puddles on the ground. High above his head the shell of a 1958 Mercury Turnpike Cruiser hung suspended from the steel rafters. Its twin headlights and imposing chrome grille looked down on him like an angry god ready to unleash its wrath.

On the door was a sign that read:

*We endeavor to satisfy.
If, however, you are unhappy
with your service, please put
your complaint in writing,
and shove it up your*

The last part of the sign was obscured by oil and dirt.

Jake pushed open the door and peered down the long dim corridor. He could see light escaping through another door slightly ajar at the end. Cautiously he made his way along the narrow passage, looking back over his shoulder as he went.

Shoop. Ping. Thump.

Jake stopped dead in his tracks. What the heck was that?

Shoop. Ping. Thump.

He swallowed hard and looked back down the corridor behind him. It was empty.

Shoop. Ping. Thump.

Reluctantly he dragged his feet along the tattered old carpet and continued toward the half-open door, the light from within spilling through every gap and nook into the passageway. He could see a shadow moving around inside as he squinted through the space between the door and the frame. Jake's breathing sounded a lot louder in his ears than it actually was. Eventually he raised his hand and knocked on the door.

"Ahem! Excuse me, Mr. Cortesi, could I have a quick word?"

Slowly, little by little, the door creaked open. Trepidation anchored Jake's eyes down toward his feet as the light from inside the room gradually slid across the floor of the corridor toward him. A pair of size-thirteen shiny brown brogues appeared in the doorway.

Jake lifted his head.

Franco Cortesi was a very big man. His body looked as though it was wedged in the doorway as he stood glaring at Jake. His head was bald on top with dark black hair at the sides and back. His many sovereign rings glinted in the light, his fingers slowly adjusting his red suspenders, pulling them down over his protruding stomach.

To Jake he looked like a stereotypical Italian gangster; all he was missing was a spaghetti Bolognese stain on his shirt.

In his right hand Cortesi clutched a golf club that he'd hooked over the door handle before pulling it open. His eyes were bulging and his teeth were gnashing. Jake couldn't help but get the impression he had caught him at a most inconvenient moment.

Franco Cortesi stepped to the side and motioned Jake in. It was a large room with no windows and flaky blue paint on the walls. A big mahogany desk sat in the center. A bulky pile of sacks was stacked unevenly from floor to ceiling in one corner.

Cortesi closed the door and brushed past Jake to a small pile of golf balls lying in the middle of the floor.

He picked one from the bunch, sat it down, and raised his club.

Jake watched in silence as the club hung in the air above Cortesi's shiny bald head. Just before he brought the club down, his angry eyes momentarily met Jake's.

Shoop—the club sliced through the air.

Ping—the ball rocketed toward the sacks as the club connected.

Thump—it walloped into one of the sacks with a dense thud before dropping harmlessly to the floor.

"So tell me, boy, why have you come to visit me?" Cortesi's very high-pitched voice caught Jake by surprise. He sounded as though he was wearing a thong that was two sizes too small.

"Well, I . . . err . . . it's, um . . . it's about . . ." Jake struggled to get the words out.

"This is an uninvited intwusion."

Intwusion? thought Jake. *Surely he means intrusion?*

"What is your name?"

"Jake . . . Jake Drake."

"Well, young Mister Dwake —"

"Drake!" interrupted Jake. "My name is Drake."

"Yes, Dwake! That is what I said. Are you deaf?" yelled Cortesi angrily.

Jake made a mental note not to correct a homicidal psychopath ever again.

"It takes a lot of guts to walk into my office uninvited: You are either despewate or cwazy."

"I'm despewate," replied Jake.

"What?"

"Desperate," said Jake hurriedly. "I'm desperate, not cwazy—I mean, crazy."

Cortesi stared at Jake for a long time before picking up another ball and continuing with his golf practice.

"Why are you despewate?"

"I need some help. Yesterday I got mugged at the Lochrannoch Estates, and all the money that I had was stolen. I want to get it back."

"How unfowtunate."

Shoop. Ping. Thump.

"The Lochwannoch Estates are very wough."

"Anyway"—Jake did his best to ignore the obvious speech impediment—"I thought you might know who the muggers were."

"Weally?" Cortesi replied, putting down his golf club and taking a seat at his desk. "Tell me what happened."

"Well," said Jake, taking a deep breath, "first the Dubble twins tried to take my money . . . "

"Aah, the Dubbles, I know them well. Lovely girls. Well wownded."

"Immensely well rounded," said Jake. "In fact I haven't seen a flat bit of them, but, moving on, the Dubbles didn't get my money. These two other blokes showed up, and they're the ones who robbed me."

"How much money are we talking about?" Cortesi asked quietly as he leaned across the desk to Jake.

"It was all the money I had on me; twenty pounds in total."

Cortesi's eyebrows plummeted like an elevator with its cable cut.

"Twenty pounds!" he roared. "You're bothewing me for twenty quid?"

Suddenly Jake was very aware he was standing all alone in a lunatic's office.

Cortesi calmed down again. He was looking pleased with himself for some reason.

"I think I might be able to help. These two men, was one of them weawing a short black jacket?"

"Yes," replied Jake.

"Did he have a mustache?"

"Yes."

"And the other one: Was he taller, with black hair that went stwaight back?"

"Exactly."

"His hair was so hard you could dwop a fwidge on his head and he wouldn't feel it?"

"I *knew* you'd know them!" Jake shouted.

"Was it those two standing behind you?"

"You what?" the words escaped Jake's mouth without him knowing.

He turned around slowly to see the two muggers standing directly behind him. The office door was lying wide open.

"What you might not wealize," Cortesi whispered in Jake's ear, "is that nothing from Lochwannoch gets stolen without making its way back here. These men work for me."

Jake could feel Cortesi's breath on his neck. It made him feel angry and threatened at the same time.

"This is Tweedle-Dumb," said Cortesi, pointing to the man in the short jacket, "and this is Tweedle-Dumber." Neither of the men appeared offended by Cortesi's introduction.

"I take what I like, and what I don't like, I take just for the heck of it."

Cortesi shoved Jake aside and picked up his golf club again.

Shoop. Ping. Thump. The practice continued.

Jake watched as Tweedle-Dumber walked over to the pile of sacks.

Shoop. Ping. Thump.

"Would you like to work for me, Jake Dwake?" asked Cortesi.

Shoop. Ping. Thump.

"That would depend on a few things: hours per week, promotion prospects, and the company retirement plan."

"Well, that's vewy simple to answer. The hours are lousy, pwomotion pwospects are cwap, and you won't live long enough to wetiwe."

Shoop. Ping. Thump.

"Hmmm"—Jake raised his hand to his chin—"it's very enticing, Mr. Cortesi, or can I call you Franco?"

"No," came the curt reply.

"Very well, I take it I would be starting at the bottom, which I'm guessing is still higher than Dumb and Dumber, doing what, exactly?"

"You would be a pwovider."

Shoop. Ping. Thump.

"A provider of what?"

"Of anything I like. I give you a list, and you pwovide the items on it. You could make yourself a lot of money, if you've got the guts."

"Sounds easy enough," Jake replied. "I'll take it."

Cortesi stopped in midswing, surprised by Jake's acceptance.

"Tewiffic," his voice reached a new glass-shattering level. "When can you start?"

"Right now," answered Jake confidently.

"Then welcome to the company."

Shoop. Ping. Thump.

"Mr. Cortesi, can I have a word?" Jake spoke like an overeager employee his first day on the job.

"Yes, Jake, what can I do for you?" Cortesi sighed; the verbal tennis between himself and Jake was starting to make his brain hurt.

"I'd like to give my notice."

Cortesi turned to look at Jake. His patience was wearing very thin, and Jake knew it.

"I calculate that at my basic hourly rate, plus bonus and expenses, you owe me . . ."

Cortesi threw his club down in anger.

". . . twenty quid!"

Cortesi smiled through his gnashing teeth and nodded his head to Tweedle-Dumber.

"You are a vewy clever young man, Jake Dwake . . ."

Jake listened to Cortesi with one eye on Tweedle-Dumber, who was untying one of the heavily mashed sacks.

". . . but you should wealize that even vewy clever people can come unstuck."

As the rope finally unraveled from the sack, Jake saw an unconscious man fall out and thud to the floor.

He was naked except for his underwear, which was pulled so far up his backside it looked more like dental floss than a wedgie. His hands and feet were tied behind his back, and his mouth was covered by a piece of white tape. Jake stared at him, willing him to move, to flinch, to show some sign of life. It seemed like forever had passed before the man groaned loudly, clenched his buttocks, and winced.

Jake breathed again.

"Let me intwoduce you both. Jake, this is a stwange guy; stwange guy, this is Jake. I'm afwaid stwange guy isn't very talkative today, on account of me beating him unconscious with golf balls."

Jake began to wish he'd taken Aidan's advice and forgotten the whole thing.

"I caught him stairwing at me fwom acwoss the stweet this morning. I don't like it when people stare at me."

Jake couldn't take his eyes off the crumpled heap at his feet.

"Maybe he didn't know who you were," murmured Jake. "If he did, he wouldn't have stared."

"Pwobably, but he should have been more careful. People could be looking at Fwanco Cowtesi and not even know it. They do not need to know what I look like to be fwightened of me, to know that I exist. Like God."

Cortesi stepped over his club lying on the carpet and strode quickly over to Jake.

"It appears that we have another new opening within the company that will be pewfect for you, Jake Dwake," he said, picking up the empty sack. "Maybe you would like to fill it?"

Jake stumbled back until the desk behind stopped him.

"I think it's time I was leaving, Mr. Cortesi." The cockiness had disappeared from Jake's voice.

"Alweady?" squeaked Cortesi. "But the party's just getting started! Let's play pin-the-tail on the stairwey stwange guy."

Jake slowly made his way toward the door, which Tweedle-Dumb was very kindly holding open for him.

"Wemember one thing, boy." Jake didn't look back. "The offer is still open. Cwime *does* pay!"

The door rattled shut on Cortesi's laughter and Jake found himself once again alone in the narrow passageway. He could feel himself quivering and stopping, and quivering and stopping, as if he had no control over it.

Then he realized his mobile phone was vibrating in his pocket. Jake pulled it out and started back down the corridor. A picture of Aidan looking particularly clueless flashed on the screen.

"I'm all right," Jake said, answering. "I'm just leaving."

"We thought he might have made you into da spicy meat-a ballas." Aidan's Italian accent didn't quite sound authentic. "How did it go? Did you find out who's got your money?"

"Yeah, I found out."

"Who is it?"

"Cortesi."

"Hi, Jake, it's Harvey, did you kick his butt?" Sometimes Harvey was too optimistic.

"Not quite." Jake sighed as he pushed the door open and stepped back into the garage. "I think I scared him, though."

"Really?"

"No."

"Hi, mate, it's me again." The phone was back in Aidan's hand. "At least now that you know, you can forget about it."

"I'm not forgetting about anything." Jake was defiant as he stepped out of the garage into the daylight. "I'm not just going to let it go—I'm going to pay them all back. Plan A is dead, so it's time for Plan B."

"What's Plan B?" asked Aidan.

"Haven't a clue."

"Jake, you'll never beat Cortesi."

"Well, Franco is definitely not scared of me, so it's obvious."

"What's obvious?"

Jake turned around to the sign above the garage in all of its green, white, and red glory. Just looking at the gangster's name made Jake's skin bubble with anger.

"I'll just have to find out what Cortesi *is* afraid of."

CHAPTER 5

The Lochrannoch Estates at night were not a good place to be.

The street lamps that hadn't made the acquaintance of a flying half brick struggled to light the dark expanse all around them. The pale moonlight did its best to illuminate the jagged skyline of the tenement rooftops, splashing puddles of light and shadow over the roof tiles, right across the projects.

But on the ground it was a haven of shadows and unlit corners for the muggers and the burglars and the street gangs.

Behind Jake's tenement block was a long line of abandoned garages.

The second-to-last from the end was where Jake's grandmother had kept her old Ford Fiesta. The car was long gone now, but the private parking garage remained.

Jake stood inside the dimly lit space in silence, watching the shadows under the door jostle in the moonlight. They had been there for almost three minutes, creeping around in the darkness and whispering. Twice he'd seen the handle of the metal garage door slowly turn, only to stop at the lock.

Jake looked at his watch; the time was quarter to eight, and his friends weren't due for another fifteen minutes.

"I'm telling you, there's nobody in," a voice whispered from the other side of the door. Jake recognized it.

On the wall above Jake's old desk was The Beast: a thirty-two-inch Easton BZ2K aluminum baseball bat with added foam gripping. Apparently the foam was particularly handy at reducing shock when the bat hit a baseball, but Jake couldn't vouch for that, as he had never once hit a ball with it. Instead he kept it in what looked like a rifle holder on the wall. Quietly he lifted The Beast down and crept across the garage.

The moonlit shadows continued to flicker under the door. As Jake neared it, his foot caught an empty can lying on the concrete floor.

"*Ssshh,* did you hear that?"

Jake stopped directly in front of the handle and listened.

"Put your ear to the door," the voice said. "See if you can hear anything."

Jake lifted the bat up over his shoulder, his eyes fixed on the shadow as it drew closer. When it eventually stopped moving, Jake swung the bat full force and smashed it against the door.

CLANG!!!

"Aaahh!!!"

Aluminum slammed metal, and metal burst eardrum.

Jake quickly unlocked the garage door and shoved it up over his head. Standing right behind it was his classmate and school bully Dillon MacIlvoy.

"I'm deaf, I'm deaf!" screamed Dillon's accomplice, Buster Johnston, as he rolled around on the ground.

"Beat it, Numb Nuts!" Jake yelled, swinging the bat behind his head.

Dillon MacIlvoy jumped back out of the way. He was a little taller than Jake, with a head so pointy it looked as if it had been screwed into a giant pencil sharpener. His braces glinted in the moonlight as he spat his usual venom in Jake's direction.

"I'm going to get you, Drake."

"Shut it," Jake replied unflinchingly, "or I'll flatten that head for you."

"What?" Buster Johnston picked himself up and stood rubbing the inside of his ear. (Buster wasn't his real name; it was Cyril, but he deemed the name Cyril unsuitable and set about finding one that was more in keeping with a slightly backward bully.)

"Get over here," Dillon growled at Buster.

"No, thanks," he replied, rubbing his ear like a dog with fleas. "I don't want a beer."

"What is wrong with you?"

"What?"

"I said, what's wrong with you?" snarled MacIlvoy.

"Who smells of poo?"

"What?"

"What?"

"What . . . oh, shut up." MacIlvoy's patience finally snapped. "Just punch his teeth in," he said, pointing at Jake.

"Leave him alone!" another voice broke the night air. Jake spun around to see the slender figure of Eddie Tierney emerge from the darkness and walk between himself and Buster.

"Who's on the phone?" Buster shoved his finger so far inside his ear it nearly came out the other one.

"What do you mean, leave him alone?" asked Dillon. "He nearly took Buster's head off!"

"Put the bat down, Jake, everything's cool," said Eddie. Jake gave a short flick of his head to show him he'd heard, but the bat stayed readied in the air.

"He ain't your boy anymore, Eddie," Dillon sneered. "Pick a side: them or us."

Eddie looked at Jake, but before he could answer, a faint mumble of voices rose up from behind the garages and got louder and louder the closer it came.

"Time to go," said Dillon quickly. "This isn't finished, Drake."

Jake watched as Dillon and Buster swiftly turned and ran toward the other end of the garages, the darkness swallowing them up before his eyes.

"I'd better go, too."

Jake lowered the bat to his side. He wanted to thank Eddie, but wasn't ready to forgive him for fighting with him two years ago. Not yet, anyway. Instead he just nodded his head.

As Eddie disappeared into the darkness behind Dillon and Buster, Jake heard his *own* friends turn the corner behind him.

"What are you doing with The Beast, Jake?" asked Sofia. Harvey and Aidan looked around suspiciously.

"I heard something," Jake replied without turning around, his eyes still watching for Eddie to return from the shadows.

"What was it?" Aidan asked.

"The Numb Nuts. They're gone now." Jake sighed deeply and turned to his friends. "Anyway," he said, smiling cheerily, "step into my office. I've got a mad idea I'd like you to help me with."

"It sounds dangerous," said Harvey inquisitively.

"It is."

Jake pushed the door up as high as it would go; Sofia and Aidan looked at each other in dread and stepped inside. Once Harvey was in, Jake pulled the door closed behind him and locked it.

Inside, the garage was dark and bare. Jake's best effort at making it a little more homey was telling Sofia to give it a "woman's touch." Apparently it had been her expert eye for style and flair that prompted his request, and not that Aidan and Harvey had told him to "get bent" when he asked them before her. Sofia had avoided the many modern styles available and instead chose furnishings that gave the space what she called a "rustic feel." Aidan preferred to call it "all this old junk from the dump."

Harvey spoke first, his face shadowed by the flame from a large white candle lighting the corner of the garage where he was sitting. "I brought some provisions," he said, reaching inside his jacket and pulling out a half-eaten tub of raspberry ripple ice cream.

Harvey had a habit of producing ice cream at inopportune moments. Once, in PE, he'd even hidden a cone down the front of his gym shorts, complete with chocolate sprinkles. He was officially, according to his friends, an ice cream addict.

"Nice!" Sofia's eyes lit up. "I love raspberry."

"Help yourself," Harvey offered, scooping out a hearty spoonful and gulping it down.

"Where are the spoons?" Sofia looked around the garage.

"Oh, hey, did you forget them? Bummer, but all the more for me," replied Harvey, grinning. "We got your text, Jake. Let me get this straight, dude: You want us to help you create your own godfather?"

Jake leaned back in his chair and rested his feet on an old kitchen table he used for a desk.

"Exactly," he answered.

"I think it's a great idea," said Aidan. "You fit the bill already. You're a twelve-year-old kid who lives at home with his flatulent grandmother; it's such a cliché."

Aidan's sarcasm wasn't lost on Jake, but instead of rising to the bait like he normally would, Jake simply turned to Sofia for support.

"How do you plan on pulling this off?" she asked him. "And what if Cortesi finds out?"

"I want Cortesi to find out; that's the whole point. I want him to know that there's a new badass maniac in town. That's my plan."

"That's it?" asked a bewildered Sofia.

"That is my plan!"

"I can see you're intent on doing some more crazy stuff, Jake," Aidan said, climbing from the musty old couch beside Harvey, "so if you'd just like to open the door, I'll check out of this madhouse."

Jake jumped up from his desk and cut Aidan off before he reached the door.

"Listen to me! I've thought this through. It was something Cortesi said that made me think of this, it's not just another crazy idea. I mean, I will have to pull off some crazy stuff, but the plan is sound, it will work."

Aidan took a deep breath and looked long and hard at Jake.

"What did Cortesi say?" asked Harvey.

Jake didn't understand the question.

"What are you talking about?"

"That made you come up with your plan?"

"He said people don't have to know what he looks like to be afraid of him," answered Jake, his eyes fixed on Aidan. "I kept hearing him say it over and over again in my head. Then I realized he was right; people will believe anything as long as there are enough people telling them it's true. If enough people believe a new, more powerful, more ruthless and dangerous and mental godfather is in town, then it becomes real."

"What the heck are you going to achieve by that, Jake?" asked Aidan. "What, you think Cortesi will just pack up and leave, maybe drop your twenty quid under the door on his way out of town?"

"I'm not letting him get away with it!" Jake's jawbone clenched as he spoke. "I don't know what it'll achieve with Cortesi, but I will get my money back and lots more besides."

"And how do you convince an entire housing projects that a made-up person is real?" Aidan demanded.

"We go guerrilla."

Harvey sat forward on the couch, and a look of confusion swept across his face.

"What . . . like monkeys?"

"Not just any monkeys, Harvey," answered Jake, "but ninja monkeys! We dress in black pajamas and slap our bare buttocks loudly to ward off predators."

"That's just . . . huh? . . . what?" Harvey was still struggling.

"Never mind, Harvey. Take a day off," Aidan interrupted him. "What do you have in mind, Jake?"

"Everything!" replied Jake, grinning. "First, we'll use the best form of communication known to man to get the story moving."

"We're going wireless?" asked Sofia.

"No," answered Aidan, "we're going to start a rumor, aren't we, Jake?"

Jake nodded.

"Now you're getting it. Rumor and gossip. Nothing spreads faster. But I'm going to need a logo, too."

"Maybe it's just me . . . ," began Harvey.

"It is," the others replied before he could finish.

". . . but I'm still confused. Why do you need a logo?"

"It goes like this," Jake explained. "Phase One: People hear about him. Phase Two: People read about him—this is where the logo comes in. Phase Three: People see him in action."

"I like the sound of Three," said Aidan.

Jake turned slowly toward Sofia and smiled expectantly.

"I suppose you're asking me to design a logo because of my expert eye for style and flair," she said with a small degree of resentment.

"No, actually," replied Jake, "you have the only color printer."

Aidan walked back to the corner of the garage where the candle was burning, the flame chiseling his face with light and shadow.

"I don't think this will work," he said to Jake, "but it might be fun to see how far we can take it. If you need my help, then I'll help."

"Me, too."

"Me, too."

Jake looked around at his friends.

"Thanks," he said. He felt like he wanted to say more, but didn't know what.

"Let's get one thing straight, though," added Aidan flatly. "*We* did not make up this godfather; it was your idea, Jake. If anyone comes knocking on the door, the godfather is *you*, not us."

Sofia and Harvey said nothing, which told Jake they thought the same.

"It's my fight," agreed Jake, nodding again. "If it all goes belly-up, I'm the godfather. You had nothing to do with it. OK, I need a list of all the loonies living in these projects; everyone from armed robbers to petty thieves to graffiti vandals."

"If it's loonies you're looking for, there's a mirror on the wall," said Harvey.

"Aren't you forgetting something?" asked Sofia.

"What?"

"The name of our godfather."

Jake walked back to his desk, plopped himself into his chair, and plonked his feet onto the desk.

"I've had a few ideas about that. Our godfather is really tall, with piercing green eyes and long black hair down to his shoulders. He is in his early forties but could pass for late thirties, no wife, no kids, no criminal convictions because he's always one step ahead. He never sleeps in the same place two nights running, he never gives second warnings, and he always shoots to kill. He moves without a sound, kills without emotion, and disappears without a trace. Nobody knows his first name. In his hometown of Palagonia in Sicily, the locals know him only by his surname. They call him Baresi. We'll call him the Big Baresi, and boy, is he going to have a lot of fun in Lochrannoch."

"Right," said Aidan, scratching his head. "Just a few ideas, then?"

"Yeah," Jake replied. "Now let's get this started."

CHAPTER 6

Nothing moves faster on the Lochrannoch Estates than a rumor.

You could start a rumor at the front of a bus and by the time you walked to the rear, someone would stop you and tell it straight back to you.

It took only four days for the gossips to really get behind the Big Baresi. Jake and his friends launched their con cautiously and cleverly. They didn't stand in front of large crowds to spread their story. Jake found it was best to casually mention in passing a story he'd heard about a new top dog in town.

Every time, the origin of the story changed. The more people he credited with telling the story to him, the more others seemed ready to believe it was true.

Aidan spent a large part of his time updating the loiterers on street corners. Harvey preferred spreading the news in hushed tones in stairwells and hallways, while Sofia favored whispering to old ladies she knew in every shop, church, and library.

Soon the name Baresi was on everyone's lips, and tales of his ruthless and violent viselike grip on the underworld swept through every apartment in the projects.

"What did I tell you: Plant the seed and watch it grow." Jake laughed as he huddled with his friends under the stairwell in the school corridor.

A steady succession of legs traipsed up and down the backless stairs just feet from their heads as their schoolmates made their way to their next class.

"Remember, we have to keep the stories realistic. Which one of you said Baresi was seven feet tall?" asked Jake.

Harvey, Aidan, and Sofia shook their heads and looked surprised.

"Well, I definitely heard another kid say Baresi was seven feet."

"We've created something that's running away from us," said Sofia. "People are making up their own rumors now."

"One kid told me that Baresi gouges out the eyes of his victims," recounted Aidan.

"That's such a lame story," said Jake. "Every gangster does that."

"How do you know?" asked Harvey.

"*The Gangsters' Pocket Guide,* page 112, chapter five, paragraph nine, titled: 'You've Whacked a Guy, Now What Do You Do?'"

Harvey was flabbergasted.

"Let me read it!"

"Not yet, dude, not yet," said Jake, trying to keep a straight face. Harvey was almost too easy to fool.

"I'll tell you an original one," said Aidan. "An old bloke at the barbershop yesterday told the geezer in the next chair that Baresi ate a Doberman because it barked outside his house all night."

"That's just weird," replied Sofia. "Someone told me Baresi can live without sleep."

"You couldn't eat a Doberman, anyway." Jake shook his head and laughed. "A Jack Russell, maybe."

Aidan raised his eyebrows. "Or a Yorkshire terrier — might be a bit hairy, mind."

"I could definitely chew my way through a Chihuahua," Harvey said very matter-of-factly. It alarmed Jake slightly but he kept quiet.

The corridors around them fell silent as the last of the stragglers hurried to their classes, leaving the hallways deserted.

"All right, we'd better get a move on." Jake nudged his friends. "And remember, stick to the truth."

"The truth is, there is no truth," Sofia replied, pulling her bag over her shoulder and stepping into the long empty hallway.

"You know what I mean," retorted Jake. "Now, is everyone still cool about tonight?"

"I'll be there," answered Harvey.

Aidan nodded as he ducked from under the stairs and stepped out beside Sofia.

"It should be fine for me, too," she said, "provided I don't get caught climbing out my window."

"Just don't wear high heels!" said Jake. "They'll be hard to move in."

"I'm not stupid." Sofia sounded peeved.

"I was talking to Aidan."

Jake grinned and headed along the corridor, leaving his friends shaking with laughter.

"Remember," he repeated, turning back, "be at the garage at three, and don't be late. We are going to have a lot of fun tonight!"

CHAPTER 7

"Quite frankly, I think you both look like a couple of plums."

Jake shone his flashlight into Aidan's and Harvey's faces, and shook his head in disbelief.

"You're enjoying this too much, Harvey. You're not going schizo on me, are you?"

Harvey wiped his lip with his sleeve.

"Listen, dude, it was dark. I thought it was black shoe polish!" he replied sternly.

"You both look like you've been trapped on a tanning bed or something."

Aidan glared angrily at Harvey, who pretended he couldn't see him.

It had been Harvey's idea to camouflage his face using his father's shoe polish, and it was he who persuaded Aidan to cover himself in it as well.

It wasn't until Jake's flashlight lit their faces that they discovered what was supposed to be Kiwi's

"Matte Black" polish was actually Body Bronzer's "Sun & Glitter" dark, fake tan.

"Look at the state of us." Aidan glowered. "We look like we've had our heads stuck up a cow's . . ."

Beep-beep. Beep-beep. Beep-beep.

Jake's text alert on his mobile phone interrupted Aidan's flow. Jake flipped the phone open and read the message.

"Sofia will be here in five minutes," he said, snapping his phone shut again.

"Let's start without her," said Harvey, pulling a balaclava down over his face so only his eyes and mouth were exposed. He looked like a bank robber with a Posh Spice tan.

"Good thinking, Harvey," said Aidan, "except Sofia's got all the gear. And another thing, why did you want to camouflage your face if you had a ski mask?"

Harvey shuffled his feet around in the dirt.

"Didn't really think of that," he mumbled.

"Genius!" muttered Aidan. It was clear to Jake that his friend was feeling pretty burnt by the whole guerrilla fake-tan affair.

An air of nervous tension hung over the entire projects. Jake looked around the side of the garages and surveyed his surroundings. There were no drunken shouts puncturing the silence, no shadows sprinting from building to building. No signs of life.

It was as if the whole of Lochrannoch had become cautious since the name Baresi had first been uttered.

"What's the time?" Harvey asked Jake.

"It's two minutes past three."

Jake leaned back against the garage wall and yawned. Harvey and Aidan stood patiently in silence, occasionally looking around to ensure no one else was watching them.

"It's really hot, isn't it?" blustered Harvey through sweaty lips. "I mean, for three o'clock in the morning."

Jake looked at him and laughed quietly. Harvey hadn't quite figured out that those two inches of fake tan he'd smothered his face in and the woolen cap were the reasons his head was frying. Jake gazed up at the night sky; it was clear, with an uninterrupted view of the full moon and all the stars.

"Do you think," Aidan began, "that right now in some far-flung corner of the earth, in a wee remote village, there are three guys looking up at the same stars?"

"Probably," Harvey replied.

"I wonder what they'd be saying."

"I can hear them," said Jake as he walked from the shadow of the garages into the moonlight. "They're saying . . . our village has lost its idiot, send Harvey. . . ."

Aidan snorted with laughter. Harvey glared at Jake.

"Meaning what exactly?" he demanded, frowning through his mask.

"*Ssshhh!* What's going on?" Sofia asked, creeping up on them. "I could hear you three halfway across the courtyard."

"Did you bring the stuff?" Jake asked her.

Sofia ignored him; she'd just clocked Aidan's face. "What the heck happened to you?" she asked in astonishment, dropping her backpack on the ground beside Jake.

"It was supposed to be black shoe polish," Aidan said through gritted teeth at Harvey. "You know, like camouflage. Turned out to be fake tan."

Sofia stifled a laugh and looked at him critically. "It's quite a deep color, isn't it? Those lotions normally last a few days."

Aidan took in a sharp breath.

"Did you hear that, Jake?" he squeaked. "A few days! I'm going to look ridiculous."

"No, you won't," Jake replied. "Just wear a little black off-the-shoulder dress and a pair of stiletto slingbacks to your physics class. Then no one will even notice your face."

Sofia giggled and opened her backpack.

"I've managed to make everything you wanted," she said to Jake. "Here are the small cards . . ."

A large, tightly bound pile of business cards landed at Jake's feet.

"The flyers . . ."

Jake picked up the business cards and shone his flashlight on them. A large red letter *B* in a fancy font adorned the front of them. Jake turned them over and read the wording on the back.

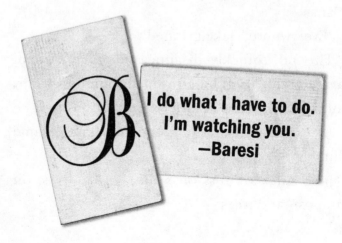

I do what I have to do. I'm watching you. —Baresi

"I still think we should have something with a bit more balls as a message," Harvey informed them. "Something like: 'I'm going to ram my fist so far down your throat, I'll punch a hole in the back of your pants.'"

"It's because you say things like that, Harvey, that your mum and dad have rubber bedsheets," replied Jake. Harvey ignored him.

Sofia continued to pull bundles of cards, flyers, and stickers from her bag.

"That's everything," she said at last, zipping up her backpack.

Jake stood looking down at the mound on the ground. All around him lay piles of paper, and all with the same bold letter on them.

"Where do you want us to put them?" asked Aidan.

"Everywhere." Jake grinned.

The pile quickly disappeared. Jake, Aidan, Harvey, and Sofia grabbed as many bundles as they could and departed in different directions.

As Lochrannoch slept, the Big Baresi came calling.

Jake stuck posters on walls, on windows, on lampposts and trees.

Aidan and Sofia stuffed flyers under doors and windshield wipers, into mailboxes and through open windows.

Harvey stuck stickers anywhere and everywhere.

Slowly but surely the big red *B* descended on Lochrannoch like a paper blanket. Soon there wasn't a single square foot of Lochrannoch left uncovered.

Jake looked down at his watch; it was nearly five o'clock and the darkness was beginning to fade. All around him Lochrannoch was swathed in a sea of Baresi. It had taken them almost two hours to coat an entire pubic housing projects in paper, but they'd managed it. Jake clutched the very last flyer in his hand and smiled. The sheer exhaustion of his night's slog and the speed at which he had been working was beginning to show. His shoulders drooped with tiredness as he turned to the last mail slot. Slowly it creaked open and he dropped the flyer onto the carpet inside. Suddenly the hall light inside the apartment flicked on, and Jake watched a large figure pound toward him through the bubbled glass in the door.

Jake turned quickly and ran to the corner stairwell, hiding in the fading shadows.

He watched in silence as the door squeaked open, and a bulky man in his boxer shorts and undershirt stepped onto the doorstep in his bare feet.

A noise screeched out across the courtyard, catching Jake by surprise. The man was whistling at the top of his lungs.

"Is he there?" Jake heard a muffled woman's voice inside the apartment.

"Can't see him," the man replied before letting rip with another ear-bursting whistle.

Jake noticed that a piece of paper had become stuck under the man's toes. He watched anxiously as the man lifted his foot and picked it off. It was the Baresi flyer Jake had just dropped through his door.

"Baresi?" the man mumbled in a state of confusion.

Just then Jake heard a strange rustling noise coming up the stairs, getting closer and closer. Jake looked for a way out, but the huge man in his boxer shorts stood blocking his exit. The rustling quickly became louder. Whatever it was was climbing the stairs at a rapid rate. Jake had nowhere to go — he held his breath as the noise rounded the last flight of stairs and came right for him. He gritted his teeth and closed his eyes.

The noise went straight past.

Jake opened one eye in surprise. He was alone again in the stairwell. As he turned back, he noticed a long-haired dog plastered in Baresi stickers running toward the man. The stickers covered its body from ears to tail, and everywhere else in between.

Mental note, Jake thought. *If you get out of this, kill Harvey.*

"What the . . . ?" The man stood in astonishment as his border collie crackled and scrunched before him.

"Who in the world did that to Skipper?" the woman's voice shouted from behind the window of the apartment.

"Some guy called Baresi," the man hollered back, his face contorted with anger, "and when I get my hands on him, I'll snap him in two!"

CHAPTER 8

"I'm having twouble descwibing just how angwy I feel wight now."

Franco Cortesi was not in a good mood. His voice seemed even squeakier than normal.

The ceiling light above his bald head shone down brightly, making the surface of his scalp gleam, as he sat behind his desk holding his face in his hands.

"Wemind me what it is I pay the police for," he said, glowering through his fingers at the two men standing opposite his desk. Both of them looked at each other, but neither replied.

"Please tell me, Detective Chief Inspector Stone, what leads you have on this Bawesi chawacter."

"Baresi is a very slippery man," the detective replied, "but we will track him down."

Chief Stone was one of the most highly decorated police officers in Glasgow. He was also one of the most corrupt, and spent more time protecting those criminals who paid him than arresting them.

"We've got all of our snitches with their ears to the ground," he continued, sweeping his gray hair across his head into the widest of side partings. The buttons on his vest looked like they might ping off at any minute, like a button machine gun, as they struggled to hold back his bulging belly.

"All of your snitches are wunning scared." Cortesi slammed his fists down hard on the desk.

Stone didn't flinch, but his colleague Officer Keith Surpress shook a little.

"Appawently Bawesi is watching evewyone."

"No one seems to know what Baresi looks like," Surpress complained. "It's a bit difficult trying to find a ghost."

Surpress shuffled his feet uneasily. He tried to act assured in front of Cortesi, but only managed to look anxious. His slender frame stooped as he spoke, like a man not entirely comfortable with taking orders from crooks. He didn't appear to have any problems taking their money every month, however.

"Rest assured we will find Baresi," said Stone soothingly. "We're speaking to the Italian authorities and they're helping us identify who he is and locate where he comes from. They have no file on him — whoever Baresi is, he's good. But we'll nail him, don't you worry."

"I'm vewy glad to hear it. I would hate to have to show you the limits of my patience." Cortesi leaned back in his recliner and looked up at the ceiling.

"Evewywhere I go I see the name Bawesi, evewy person I speak to talks to me about Bawesi. Bawesi, Bawesi, Bawesi. All day long. I hate Bawesi."

Officer Surpress just managed to stifle a giggle — luckily for him Cortesi ranted on, blissfully unaware.

"And what is it with his widiculous calling cards, they're evewywhere. Do you think I should get a card?"

Chief Stone and Officer Surpress were unsure how to answer.

"No, that's a silly idea," Cortesi continued, answering his own question, "but if I did, my card would be much pwettier than his. Once you find out who Bawesi is and we kill him, I don't want to hear his name again."

"Here's a different name for you," said Stone, smirking. "John Joseph Scullen."

Cortesi brought his recliner up slowly until it was back in its normal position, and frowned.

"What about Scullen?"

"He got out of jail over a week ago. The cabbie who dropped him off said he brought him back to the Lochrannoch Estates."

"That's vewy intewesting information." Cortesi reached into his drawer and pulled out a fat cigar. "And why do you think he came back to Lochwannoch?" He flicked his lighter and soon small wisps of smoke escaped from his nose as he puffed furiously on his cigar, clearly troubled.

"We think he came back for the diamonds," replied Officer Surpress.

"What diamonds?"

"The diamonds from the heist."

"I wonder why he thinks I still have the diamonds," Cortesi said thoughtfully.

"I guess he figures you had too much heat so you couldn't sell them," said Stone. "We are talking about one and a half million pounds' worth — that's three million dollars on the global market. You should ask yourself whether your diamonds are safe right now."

"By the way," added Surpress nonchalantly, "where are you hiding them?"

Cortesi sucked hard on his cigar and blew the smoke across the desk at them both.

"My diamonds are safe," he replied, eyeing the policemen suspiciously. "Besides, it wasn't me who awwested Scullen and made certain he took all the blame. I didn't testify in court and send him to jail. How do you know he hasn't come back for you two?"

"I doubt even Scullen is stupid enough to come after two cops." Stone sneered at the very thought. "As soon as we have anything worth telling you, we'll report back."

Both officers turned and walked toward the door of the office.

"When you go out, tell Dumb and Dumber to come see me," Cortesi shouted after them. "If they can dwag themselves away fwom those Dubble girls, of course. They're like love-stwuck teenagers."

Stone emerged first from the darkness of the garage into the bright sunshine and pulled on his sunglasses. Outside, the two men who had mugged Jake stood joking with Demi and Desiree Dubble.

"Oi! He wants to see you both," shouted Stone without so much as a sideward glance.

And instantly Cortesi's men scurried inside.

* * *

"Have you seen anyone stwange hanging awound wecently?" Cortesi questioned his goons.

Both Tweedle-Dumb and Tweedle-Dumber shook their heads.

"Well, keep an eye out. John Joseph Scullen is out of jail and back in Lochwannoch. That's all I need wight now with this Bawesi business."

"No problem, Boss," they both said in unison.

"And if you hear anything about Bawesi, I want to know stwaightaway."

The taller of the two men coughed nervously.

"Well, Boss, I have heard something about Baresi. I mean, it's not really about Baresi, but in a way it is . . ."

"Spit it out, you bwainless idiot," snapped Cortesi impatiently.

"It's about Mickey Chang . . ."

"Mickey Chang from the Southside? What does he want?"

"Some of his guys have been over at the projects asking questions about Baresi. Chang thinks you're losing your grip."

"Losing my gwip!" Cortesi screamed. "I'm not losing my gwip; I have a firm gwip!"

"I'm just telling you what I've heard, Boss."

71

Cortesi jumped angrily from his chair and paced the floor like a man demented.

"First Bawesi and now Mickey Chang!" he growled under his breath. "I'll kill them both. No wait, Fwanco, wait. You have to be bwainy now. . . ."

Cortesi suddenly stopped pacing and spun toward his men.

"I know! Tell Chang I want to see him. Tell him I have information that the Big Bawesi will soon be coming after him and we can stop him if we work together."

"You want to join forces with Mickey Chang?" asked Tweedle-Dumb. "But you hate Chang."

"Yes, of course I do," replied Cortesi, "but I would much pwefer he was inside my tent peeing out, than outside my tent peeing in. If you know what I mean."

The bewildered expressions on his goons' faces told Cortesi they didn't.

"Just set up a meeting!" he snarled. "Between us we will find this Bawesi person, whoever he is, and kill him!"

"Do you think Scullen is still hanging around?" asked Surpress as he slammed the car door shut and pulled on his seat belt.

"Scullen isn't going anywhere without Cortesi's money," replied Stone sharply. "It's the reason he's back here."

"Do you think he has anything to do with this Baresi guy?"

"I've thought about it, and I think it's too much of a coincidence — him coming back the same time this Baresi shows up. I think they're working together. So our job is simple."

"What do you mean, simple?" asked Surpress.

"Find Baresi and we'll find Scullen. Then we kill them both."

"And Cortesi?"

"We'll let Scullen find the jewels first, and when we whack him we'll whack Cortesi as well. Just say they both did each other."

Surpress smiled and pulled away.

Farther up the road a silver Volkswagen Golf leaned heavily toward the driver's side. As Stone and Surpress passed by, the large shaven head of John Joseph Scullen rose up warily from the driver's seat. His eyes followed the police car in his mirror as it disappeared over the hill behind him. When it had gone, he turned his attention back to Cortesi's garage. He gripped the steering wheel tightly as he stared through the open garage doors and into the darkness beyond.

It wasn't until the leather trim on the steering wheel burst at the seams that the blood finally seeped back into his fingers and he drove quietly away.

CHAPTER 9

Larry Jarvis was a car thief, an armed robber, a receiver of stolen goods, a con man, a mugger, a burglar, a grievous bodily harmer, a criminal enforcer, and most nights after a heavy drinking session, a disturber of the peace.

While the rest of the Lochrannoch Estates were treading uncertainly in the Big Baresi's shadow, Larry Jarvis simply shrugged an arrogant shrug and went about his criminal activities.

Two days had passed since Jake and the others had covered the projects with the name Baresi, and although nobody outwardly admitted it, everyone felt the unease in the air.

People's eyes flicked nervously as they passed one another in the street, glancing edgily over their shoulder for a sign that the Big Baresi was watching them.

I do what I have to do. I'm watching you. —Baresi.

The words that had appeared all over the projects' walls and windows were etched in the minds of the Lochrannoch inhabitants as they cautiously got on with their lives.

The obvious exception was Larry Jarvis.

He was very near the top of Jake's short list of lowlifes and jerks.

The door of his second-floor apartment banged shut. He continued on toward the elevator, laughing into his cell as he went.

"I don't give two hoots what these stupid bloody cards are saying. Tell Mr. Cortesi that as far as I'm concerned it's business as usual."

The down arrow lit up as Jarvis pressed the button, and the elevator descended from the eleventh floor above him.

"I mean, who the heck is this little Italian pretty boy, Baresi? Has anyone actually caught sight of him?"

The elevator passed the seventh floor.

"I hear Fingers McGraw isn't taking it seriously, either. Mind you, that thick little rat wouldn't stop thieving if you chopped his bloody arms off."

Jarvis turned to look out the hall window as the elevator doors pinged open behind him.

"I'm telling you, this Baresi knows better than to mess with me." He smirked confidently as he turned and paced toward the doors. "He'd better watch his step."

As his foot hit the metal floor, a bright electrical flash illuminated the shaft, and the elevator doors suddenly snapped shut behind him.

Instantly the lights died and the elevator was in darkness.

Jarvis dropped his phone and stared up through the open roof panel into the dark expanse above him. "Hello . . . is there anybody there . . . ?" His voice trailed off suspiciously as he yelled.

A sliver of light shone through the open doors on the fifth floor high above, where Jake and Aidan lay on their bellies, peering over the edge.

"I hope you're right about this, Jake," said Aidan anxiously. "The coppers don't take kindly to people sabotaging elevators."

"Relax," Jake whispered, gazing down. "I'll have the power back on in a minute."

Aidan pulled three large burlap sacks across to the open door.

"This stuff smells disgusting," he said, wincing away from the stink. "Worse than one of your grandma's . . . "

"Watch out!" Jake interrupted.

"Who's up there? I can hear somebody

whispering!" the angry voice boomed up the shaft.

Larry Jarvis stood in darkness in the center of the elevator, looking up through the gap in the metal roof. Above his head, the sliver of light from the fifth floor gradually widened as Jake and Aidan pried the doors farther open.

"Oi, look, the power's gone off, can you get help?" yelled Jarvis.

Neither boy replied.

"Get ready," Jake whispered to Aidan. "Three, two, one, bombs away!"

Jarvis jumped up and grabbed the ledge of the open panel, pulling his head up through the gap to see if he could climb out.

There was an enormous *whoosh*. Rushing down the shaft toward him was a shower of horse dung and dog and cat turds kindly donated by the neighborhood's pets.

Larry Jarvis was hit full in the face. "Aargh!" he yelled. He let go of the edge of the escape hatch and fell back into the elevator car followed by three sack loads of manure.

"I'm going to kill you!" he screamed up the shaft, coughing dung from his mouth and violently slapping turds from his face and hair.

All of a sudden the light above him fragmented as hundreds of cards sailed down the shaft toward him, twirling and spinning, flapping and twisting. They sounded like a hundred moths trapped in a tin can.

"My God, the stench! I'm covered in crap . . . ! That's it! I'm going to rip out your spleen!" The venom spilled from Jarvis's mouth as the cards landed all around him. "I'm going to murder you, do you hear me?"

The light above his head slowly disappeared as the doors slid together, closing with a *thunk!* The last of the cards flapped to a rest and Jarvis was alone in the silence of the empty elevator shaft.

Reaching into his pocket, he pulled out a cigarette lighter and flicked it on. Picking up a card, he slowly brought it to the naked flame, illuminating a large red letter *B* and the immortal words: *I'm watching you.*

"Baresi!" he exclaimed, nearly choking on the name.

Jarvis wearily dropped the lighter and slouched against the wall. The flame died and went out.

"Baresi?" he muttered again. "Oh, great."

CHAPTER 10

Word of Larry Jarvis's unfortunate elevator incident didn't just spread around the projects, it also made it as far as a local radio news report and a small side-column mention in the *Daily Record* newspaper.

"Attempted Murder in Elevator Shaft," blared the headline. "Villain Is Victim in Vicious Attack."

Aidan slapped the newspaper down onto the desk in front of Jake.

"Read it!" he yelled angrily. "'Attempted murder,' it says! You never mentioned anything about attempted murder!"

"It was accidental, Aidan, you were there," Jake replied as he got up and walked past Harvey and Sofia on the couch to close the garage door.

"Exactly, I was there. That makes me an accomplice: an accomplice to an attempted murder."

"It was accidental!" repeated Jake.

"Silly me, of course, you're right," said Aidan gently. "We'll just say yes, we did cut the elevator cable, but only to badly hurt and frighten the man, not to kill him. That'll get us off the hook—*I don't think!*"

"Dude, you're not *on* the hook."

"And you can shut up for a start!" Aidan was in no mood to be placated by Harvey.

"What was it they wrote about your handiwork? Let me see. . . ."

Aidan quickly scanned through the pages of the paper. "Ah yes, here it is: 'Cat Flattened by Falling Toaster in High-Rise Horror'! You killed a poor little kitty, Harvey."

"It wasn't my fault, dude; the cat wasn't the target. I was aiming for a mugger's car."

"What made you lob a toaster off the rooftop?" Sofia asked in astonishment. "Wasn't there something easier?"

"It seemed like a good idea at the time. I got up on the roof and saw an old toaster oven that had been left lying there. It was in exactly the right place, so I tipped it over the edge and down toward the car. It landed bang on top of it."

"To be fair," Sofia said reasonably, "how was Harvey to know there was a cat in the car?"

"The cat wasn't in the car—it was in the toaster!"

"Oh." Sofia shook her head despairingly.

"This is getting out of control, Jake," Aidan continued. "Attempted murders, cat killers, and the name Baresi is all over the news."

"Stop sweating; it's all going according to plan."

"What plan?" argued Aidan. "You don't have a plan—you're just having fun."

"What's wrong with enjoying your work?" replied Jake. "Just simmer down for a second and stop acting like you should be wearing a bra. No offense, Sofia."

Sofia shrugged.

"The more headlines the Big Baresi gets, the more Cortesi is going to believe he really does exist. The more he believes it, the more paranoid he's going to get. Then we'll get rid of *him* for good."

"How?" Aidan demanded. "How exactly do we get rid of him?"

"It's a surprise."

"Yeah, right."

"I'm not sure if that was an argument or a statement," joked Jake. "Just trust me."

Aidan remained unconvinced.

"I agreed to do this with you, Jake, because I thought it would be a laugh, and it was, to start with, but now it's getting out of hand and it's not funny anymore."

Jake rocked backward on his chair and sighed.

"Do you want to bail on us now, Aidan? If you do, I won't try and talk you out of it."

Aidan looked down and shuffled his feet, then glanced across the garage at Harvey and Sofia.

"I'm just saying we need to be careful," he murmured.

"OK, fair enough," Jake conceded. "From this moment on we won't do anything stupid or reckless — no more wild stuff. Is that better?"

After a momentary pause, Aidan nodded in agreement.

"Dude, what if you've already started to do something a bit wild, are you allowed to finish it?" asked Harvey, sort of sheepishly.

Jake rolled his eyes toward the roof.

"What the heck have you done now, Harvey?"

CHAPTER 11

The truck's massive front wheels spun in the soft dirt and gravel, and black diesel smoke belched from its side exhaust pipe.

It lurched out of the warehouse in short bursts, like an overexcited puppy straining at its leash, eager to get ahead.

Behind the cab, the truck's long blue trailer groaned under the strain as it jerked along, the loud engine revs echoing from what was left of the corrugated metal walls. The sunlight was fading fast behind the warehouse as the truck was coaxed through the doors into the expansive wasteland outside and turned down the disused drive toward the side street.

"I thought you said you could drive!" shouted Sofia as Jake struggled to get the truck into gear.

He could reach the pedals without much effort, but changing gear with the necessary *off* accelerator — *on* clutch — *in* gear — *off* clutch — *on* accelerator procedure was much harder than he had thought it would be.

"Belt up!" he growled, twirling the large steering wheel in his hands.

"My seat belt is already on, thank you," Sofia replied, pulling the strap out from her chest so Jake could see.

"I meant your mouth."

"Jake, I have a very bad feeling about this," Aidan whimpered, bouncing around on the bench seat at the back of the cab with Harvey.

"Me, too," agreed Jake. "I lied. I can't drive."

The truck swept out onto a two-lane highway, the trailer snaking wildly for a few hundred feet before Jake finally steadied it and kept it pointing straight.

"Sofia, could you do something for me, please?" said Jake coolly. "Remind me to kick Harvey's arse."

Harvey frowned, but considering he had got them into their current predicament with the truck, he knew better than to argue.

"How the heck did you manage to drive this rig, anyway?" Aidan asked him in astonishment. Harvey ignored the question and did his best to act blasé, which only highlighted his awkwardness.

Jake swung the truck right at a traffic circle, leaving the highway behind. Up ahead, a bridge loomed into view. A red and white sign flashed past as they careered down the road toward the crossing.

"What did that sign say?" Jake asked.

"It said, 'Maximum height: fifteen feet,'" Sofia answered.

"Fair enough."

A horrible silence filled the cab.

"How high is this truck?" Aidan shouted over Jake's shoulder.

"We'll soon find out," Jake shouted back, then swallowed. Hard.

A small row of shops trembled as the truck thundered past. Inside, shopkeepers and customers alike raced to the windows to glimpse the enormous rig hurtling down the road toward the small railroad bridge at the bottom.

"I don't think we're going to make it!" quavered Sofia, pulling back into her seat.

"We'll make it," Jake declared without hesitation, thumping his foot down harder on the accelerator. Instantly the pitch of the engine climbed as the truck gathered speed. Harvey sat openmouthed with terror as the bridge began to fill the windshield.

"We're going to hit it!" screamed Aidan.

The stick shift shuddered as Jake crunched it into a higher gear, demanding more speed.

"We'll be fine!" he yelled back doggedly as the speedometer climbed and the needle touched fifty miles per hour.

The cars and vans on the opposite side of the road started flashing their headlights in warning, but Jake ignored them and stomped down even harder on the pedal. The bridge got closer and closer and closer.

"We're not going to make it!" all three of his friends screamed in unison.

The blood drained from Jake's knuckles as his hands gripped the wheel as tight as they could, his eyes wide and fixed determinedly on the bridge.

"Oh, sh . . . !" he shouted. "We're not going to make it!"

The truck's rear wheels locked as Jake jumped on the brakes. Smoke belched from between the tires as concrete burned rubber and the truck started to skid toward the bridge. Jake pushed down on the brake pedal as hard as he could, trying to slow the massive three-ton rig.

"We're going to hit!" yelled Jake, before screaming at the top of his lungs. The others joined in even louder.

The cab slipped beneath the bridge, but the top of the trailer slammed into the stone parapet, throwing them forward before their seat belts locked and held them in their seats.

Tortured metal screeches filled the air as the truck continued to slide, dragging the trailer behind it. The stone parapet peeled back the metal roof like the lid of a can of sardines, until the rig finally shuddered and groaned to a halt, a few feet out the other side of the bridge.

The metal skin of the roof was concertinaed at the back, leaving three quarters of the trailer exposed to the open air.

Inside the cab, Jake slowed his breathing back to normal and lessened his grip on the wheel. The engine continued to idle, rumbling gently.

Sofia sat staring through the windshield in a state of shock. Jake turned to ask her if she was OK, but she simply pushed her hand toward his face and motioned him not to speak.

"I told you we'd make it through," joked Jake, turning to Harvey and Aidan in the back. Harvey stared straight through him with a catatonic expression on his face, as if he'd just been cryogenically frozen.

"This is all your fault, Jake," muttered Aidan. His breathing was heavy and labored, but Jake was unsure whether it was from anger or shock.

"Don't start, Aidan," Jake replied. "That's all I need; and, anyway, it's all Harvey's fault."

"My fault?" Harvey suddenly snapped out of his cryogenic state. "Dude, you just nearly killed us, you stupid plonker."

"Oh, so I'm the plonker, am I? You stole this truck, then hid it in your own uncle's warehouse. Very clever, I don't think."

"I told you, it was Fingers McGraw who stole it. I just stole it back, otherwise Cortesi would have sold it."

"Jake . . . ," Sofia tried to interrupt.

"If you hadn't stolen it, you wouldn't have needed to hide it, if you hadn't hidden it, we wouldn't have had to move it, you blockhead!"

"Jake . . . ," Sofia persevered.

"If you hadn't crashed it through a bridge, I wouldn't have peed my pants!"

Aidan looked at Harvey's pants, and then slid toward the end of the seat.

"Shut up, both of you!" yelled Sofia. "There are two policemen running toward us!"

Jake spun around to see two uniformed officers racing across the street. The noise of the crash had enticed a small crowd of women out onto the pavement, gasping and shaking their heads.

"What do we do now?" panicked Jake.

"Get us out of here," yelled Aidan.

The crunch of the gears startled the onlookers as Jake slammed the stick shift into first and hammered the accelerator. Instantly the truck lurched forward and sped away from the bridge, toward an intersection with the two-lane highway ahead.

The police officers turned and sprinted back toward their car as the truck thundered past them with Jake at the wheel.

Another crunch of the gears and the truck summoned more power and speed. The highway drew steadily closer.

"Shouldn't we be slowing down if we're going to make a turn?" Sofia asked as she looked on in horror.

"You would think so, wouldn't you?" replied Jake before slamming into a higher gear and increasing the speed.

The flashing blue lights of the police car swerved in and out of Jake's side-view mirror as the driver clung to his tail.

"Hang on!" yelled Jake as the truck hurtled toward the YIELD sign at the end of the road. When the truck reached the junction with the highway, Jake suddenly pulled down hard on the steering wheel, sending the rig lurching around the corner, the weight of the trailer and the speed of the turn lifting the tires off the road on one side.

Harvey, Aidan, and Sofia screamed as the whole of the cab leaned as though it was going to fall over. Horns blared as cars were forced to swerve and brake hard to avoid a collision. Jake grappled ferociously with the steering wheel, which was threatening to tear his arms from their sockets; then with a high-pitched squeal the airborne tires on the side of the trailer found the concrete again, and Jake was back in control.

The police car skidded around the bend behind them, lights flashing and siren wailing.

"Perhaps we should pull over," suggested Aidan.

Jake's eyes flicked toward him in the rearview mirror.

"Terrific idea. Do you want to do the explaining or shall I?"

The blue lights in Jake's mirror quickly tripled as another two police cars joined the chase.

Jake saw brake lights illuminate in front of him as cars backed up in the rush hour congestion. He swung the steering wheel, and the truck swerved onto the hard shoulder, racing past the traffic that had slowed to a crawl on the main highway.

"We need to get off this road," said Jake as he watched the police cars follow him past the slow-moving traffic.

"Why don't we just tell them that the Big Baresi is at the wheel, Jake?" Aidan suggested sarcastically. "Maybe they'll get scared and stop chasing us!"

Jake ignored him.

Dirt and stones were being kicked into the air by the truck's wide tires, pinging off the windshields of the police cars behind, which were still determinedly giving chase.

Jake steered the rig off the hard shoulder and down the first exit ramp he passed, leaving the long line of tightly packed cars to watch the high-speed chase unfolding.

The road bent into a sweeping right-hand turn that doubled under the highway and carried them away from the jammed traffic, but the police sirens continued to wail as the cars pursued them, refusing to give up.

"I have to get these cops off our tail!" cried Jake.

"*I* know," replied Aidan, "let's look out for a bus stop. Maybe if we're quick enough, we can hide this eighteen-wheeler inside it." He sat back in his seat and shook his head.

"My mum and dad are going to kill me for this," Harvey suddenly shouted, as if he'd just realized the severity of the situation, "and that's not a euphemism; they will literally kill me!"

"This is crazy!" Aidan yelled.

"I know!" Jake shouted back. "I can't believe Harvey said 'euphemism,' either."

The truck rolled over the top of a hill at a frightening speed, but behind it the police cars kept pace.

As the weight of the rig pushed them faster down the other side, Jake shifted gear and stomped his foot down harder on the accelerator. The engine whined, the needle on the tachometer swung to the red line, and the truck somehow summoned more power from somewhere.

At the bottom of the hill, the road curved and took them straight back toward the busy streets of the city.

The police sirens echoed off shops and buildings as Jake thundered through the narrow streets, still struggling to come to grips with the size of the rig, blue lights chasing him all the way.

"We're not getting away from them, Jake. Just give up now!" pleaded Aidan.

For a split second Jake glanced at him in the mirror, then turned his attention back to the road. Directly in front of him, a young mother edged her small car from a parking space out onto the street, blissfully unaware of the danger hurtling toward her and her baby.

"Look out!" yelled Jake as he jumped on the brakes and spun the steering wheel.

The eighteen-wheeler careered across the oncoming traffic and plowed through the side wall of the Yum Yum Bubble Gum Factory.

Sofia screamed as the truck smashed through concrete support pillars, throwing plumes of white dust into the air.

Behind them the police cars were forced into the same evasive measure, and one after the other they skidded through the devastation behind the truck.

Jake clutched at the steering wheel. The tractor trailer plowed through the reception area with ridiculous ease, smack into the belly of the factory. Huge bowl blenders vibrated loudly, their large rotating blades mixing bubble gum base with sweeteners and flavorings, as Jake hurtled past and through the center of the production line.

Workers screamed and ran from their workstations, diving through the nearest exit doors. The sirens were getting louder and louder. In a matter of seconds the police cars were skidding into the now almost-abandoned factory, their tires squealing against the pristine white floor tiles.

"What are you doing, Jake?" screamed Sofia, as Jake swerved the truck and clipped one of the huge blender containers.

"Trying to get us out of here!" he yelled back.

The container rocked on its stand, the bubble gum concoction swirling and swishing inside it, until eventually the stand buckled and the vat of sticky liquid fell on its side. Hot gum gushed out across the factory floor behind the rig, thick as molten lava.

"Mmmm." Harvey stuck his head out the window and sniffed loudly. "Blueberry flavor."

The first police officer could see a hot sticky catastrophe flooding toward him. He jumped on his brakes and his car tires squealed, leaving long trails of black rubber on the gleaming floor. As the officer stamped helplessly on the pedals, the car slid head-on into the flow of liquid gum and spun in circles, spraying multicolored goo high in the air.

The second officer in pursuit twirled his steering wheel, just managing to avoid his colleague, and spun his car away from the mess. Jake watched in his mirror as the squad car disappeared through the center of a large sheet of newly made gum stretched between huge steel rollers, shredding it to bits. Strips of pink confectionary fell from the rollers, burying the car completely.

Jake yanked down hard on the steering wheel and the truck swung left and then right at the back of the factory.

"Quick question," said Aidan anxiously. "Where are you going, Jake?"

"I told you; I'm getting us out of here!" Jake shouted back, concentrating hard.

"Yes, but *how* are we going to get out of here?" Sofia panicked.

"The same way we came in," Jake replied, accelerating up the other side of the production line.

A third police car swerved in front of the truck. Jake clipped its rear end and sent it spinning across the factory floor, straight into the front of a large heating generator, cracking its pipes. Smoke billowed from the damaged machine.

Jake brought the truck to a shuddering halt.

"Why are you stopping, Jake?" asked Aidan nervously. "We have to get out of here!"

Jake didn't reply; his heart was beating so fast he felt like he might flatline as he looked out the side window at the wrecked car.

"I need to make sure the cops are OK," he eventually blustered through sweat-drenched, anxious lips.

The cloud of smoke from the generator's fractured pipes made its way toward the roof of the factory. Eventually it reached the smoke alarms and the factory's sprinklers sprayed into life, reducing mounds of gum to soft stretchy mush.

"I think we'd better get out of here," Sofia muttered as the doors to the police car opened and two very angry-looking officers emerged from inside.

Jake crunched the gears, trying hard to force the stick shift into first. The engine revved high as he pressed the accelerator, but with no gear selected, the truck remained stationary, the heavy whine from its engine echoing off the stark walls.

"Come on, come on!" Jake yelled, struggling with the gearshift.

The officers were approaching the truck, fast.

Jake planted his foot harder on the accelerator, but the mass of bubble gum piling up on the floor was now so water-soaked it began to resemble a viscous multicolored sea. Within seconds it had risen so high that it enveloped the truck's exhaust pipe. As Jake revved the engine, a large bubble began to appear, and the harder Jake pressed, the bigger the bubble became.

"This doesn't look good," said Aidan, flabbergasted, watching the huge bubble rising up the side of the cab.

The two policemen stopped running and stood openmouthed.

"Ladies and gentlemen," announced Jake as the enormous exhaust-powered bubble rose twenty feet in the air above them, "please adopt the brace position and prepare for a big bang."

The two officers edged backward, and Jake gave one last hard prod of the pedal. . . . Instantly the bubble exploded. A ground-trembling bang shook the factory. Jake scrambled up from the bottom of the cab and looked out the window.

The two policemen had been blown against one wall and were stuck fast by the world's biggest bubble-gum bubble! They were coated in thick pink bubble gum, their feet dangling above the ground.

Harvey eventually broke the silence in the cab. "Dudes, is it just me or can everyone else see two coppers stuck to the wall with gum?"

"Yeeeees," mumbled his friends in disbelief.

"Cool," Harvey wheezed. "I thought I was cracking up."

Jake felt the gentle thrum of the truck's engine pulse through his fingers as he gripped the wheel. With one loud crunch from the transmission, he managed to find first gear and edge the truck slowly back down the factory floor, away from the fruit-flavored chaos he had caused, through the mangled reception area, and back out onto the street.

In the distance, more sirens could be heard as police cars steadily picked their way through the congestion and the commotion, toward the factory.

Jake crunched the gears again and rolled the truck in the other direction, through stunned pedestrians and commuters, past cars full of astounded passengers, down toward the end of the street.

With a loud engine rev and a burst of diesel smoke, the truck disappeared around the corner and out of sight.

* * *

Aidan pulled down the long steel shutters behind the truck as Jake rolled it to a stop inside the warehouse.

Steam belched from inside the engine and curled up toward what was left of the windshield. Sofia and Harvey stood on the small loading dock and surveyed the damage. Behind them a tattered COWELL'S FRUIT MARKET sign hung lopsided from the wall.

"You know what?" said Jake, climbing down from the cab. "I bet we got lucky and nobody even noticed."

The engine cover dropped off and clanged to the ground at his feet, and a large puddle of oil crept out toward his sneakers.

"But then again . . ."

"Do you think what just happened is funny, Jake?" Aidan's tone couldn't be construed as anything other than rage.

"Give me a break, Aidan." Jake sighed. "Nobody was hurt, and we got the truck out of Harvey's uncle's warehouse. We've taken it to this safer warehouse. Job done."

"It might have escaped your attention, Einstein, but there is the small matter of hundreds of grands' worth of damage!"

Jake rubbed his tired eyes and looked toward the heavens.

"Dude, are you sure this place is safe?" asked Harvey.

Jake was almost too worn out to reply. "I think so, but I don't know for sure. It's been derelict for years. It's supposed to be getting knocked down in a month's time. It should be all right for a few days, anyway."

Aidan spoke through gritted teeth. "Today was the last day I had anything to do with Baresi. From now on I'm out. I don't want to see, hear, or speak that stupid name ever again." He turned and walked quickly toward the warehouse doors.

Sofia and Harvey looked at each other, unsure whether to follow Aidan or stay with Jake.

"I've got just one question, Aidan," Jake yelled after him.

Aidan didn't look back.

"Don't you want to know what's in the back of the truck?"

Aidan's stride began to slow, from purposeful to pondering until eventually it came to a stop.

"Oh, how I hate you," he muttered loud enough for Jake to hear.

Jake smiled.

* * *

Harvey pulled the long handle out from the door and instantly the metal dead bolt slid from its hasp with a teeth-clenching screech.

Sofia covered her ears at the sound before grabbing the trailer door and helping Harvey pull it open.

Jake stood a few feet back beside Aidan, watching in silence as the door quietly slid open in front of them.

"It's full of boxes," Sofia informed them, pushing the door as wide as it would go.

"What's in them?" asked Jake.

"I can't see from here," she replied.

"Well, climb up and have a look."

Sofia peered into the trailer. There were some signs that the boxes had previously been stacked in neat piles, but that was obviously before Jake took them for a spin. Now they just lay on top of one another in a large heap.

"I'm not getting in there," said Sofia. "There might be a dead body or something."

Jake sighed and rolled his eyes toward the ceiling with its exposed metal beams.

"Harvey, take a look."

"It's like that one dude says to the other dude in the film, Jake: He says, 'Shove it up your—'"

"Fine, I'll do it myself!" interrupted Jake. He ran and jumped up into the trailer.

It should have been dark inside, but because most of the trailer's roof had been forcibly removed when they went under the railroad bridge, Jake had no trouble looking around.

Aidan joined Harvey and Sofia at the open door as Jake disappeared behind a pile of boxes.

The three friends listened as the cardboard tore with a loud ripping sound.

"What's in it?" Sofia shouted inside.

Jake didn't answer.

"Jake? Jake, are you OK?"

"What's going on, dude?" Harvey got agitated.

A loud hiss suddenly filled the air inside the trailer. Instinctively Aidan, Harvey, and Sofia took a step back.

"What the heck is that?" asked Sofia.

"I don't know," replied Aidan. "Jake, are you OK?"

Suddenly something dropped down beside them from the roof of the trailer, straight on top of Harvey. His high-pitched squeals bounced off the warehouse walls as he fell back beneath it.

"Help! Get it off me!" he screamed at the top of his lungs.

The thing suddenly shot into the air, and as Harvey looked up he saw Jake standing over him, holding it above his head.

"*Konnichiwa,*" said Jake.

Harvey could hear Aidan and Sofia laughing but wasn't sure where they were.

"I would like to introduce you to Mister Inflatable Sumo Suit."

Harvey looked up at what Jake was holding above him; it was a self-inflating sumo suit and more than twice the size of Jake.

"Oh, very funny," grumbled Harvey as he picked himself up.

Aidan and Sofia appeared at his side, still giggling.

"There's boxes upon boxes of sumo suits inside," said Jake. "Thousands of them."

"They're so cool," Aidan replied. "I'm taking one."

"Good," said Harvey, "now can I get out of these pants?"

"That's not all I found." Jake bounced the sumo suit onto the ground and walked back toward the door of the trailer. "You won't believe what else is in there."

Jake reached behind the door and lifted out a flat metal box.

"Feast your eyes on this!" He smiled as he flipped open the lid.

Inside the box lay wads of worn twenty-pound notes.

Jake watched as his friends slowly approached the box, staring at its contents in disbelief.

Aidan cleared his throat. "I've never seen so much cash," he croaked.

Jake nodded in agreement.

"How much do you think it is?" asked Sofia, her voice barely above a whisper.

"I don't know," replied Jake, "but I'm guessing Franco Cortesi is missing twenty grand right now. And to think he only owed me twenty quid."

Jake sat the box on the ground and all four of them crowded around it.

It was a long time before anyone spoke again.

"One question," Sofia finally broke the silence. "What are we going to do with all this money and all these sumo suits, Jake?"

"Make more money." He smiled. "Then we'll figure out how to spend it."

CHAPTER 12

John Joseph Scullen squeezed his hulking frame into the phone booth and yanked the door closed behind him. The booth shook violently as he maneuvered his vast body around to face the phone and lifted a coin from his pocket.

Outside, the debris from Jake's eighteen-wheeler adventure the day before was still being cleared from the busy street. A group of construction workers in hard hats stood shaking their heads at the huge gap in the Yum Yum Bubble Gum factory wall—the design feature Jake had created.

Pedestrians stood gossiping as the workers erected a temporary fence around the smashed bricks and masonry that littered the pavement from where the police had removed their crime scene tape only minutes earlier.

Scullen opened a bunched-up piece of paper with the name Mad Dog and a telephone number on it, and placed it on top of the phone.

"Excuse me, mate, are you going to be in there long?" asked a voice from outside the booth.

Scullen shuffled around to see the pasty white face of a skinny young man pressed against the glass.

"You see, my mobile has just been stolen and I need to report it missing."

Scullen shoved his face against the side of the phone booth, flared his nostrils, and snarled through gritted teeth. The young man took a step back.

"I can see you don't want to be disturbed," he quavered. "I'll just walk the two miles to the other pay phone, no problem."

Scullen watched as the young guy turned and, within six steps, went from a walk to a jog to a sprint down the street.

Scullen punched in the phone number on the paper. After only three rings it was picked up.

"Hello. Who's this?" the voice answered in a thick Cockney accent.

"Hi, M.D. It's me, Scullen."

"John Joseph, my old cell mate. How are you? What can I do for you?"

Scullen looked around the street nervously, his eyes flicked from shop window to parked car to passerby as he checked to see whether he was being watched.

"Remember what I told you — the reason why I was inside?"

"What? The gems — the diamond job?"

"Yes," replied Scullen impatiently. "Well, I'm back on my old hunting ground, and I'm chasing the stones. Now, if I manage to get them, can you help me sell them quickly? Can you set me up with a buyer?"

The voice at the other end of the line went quiet.

"Well, can you?"

"I'm sure I can put you in touch with a bloke who knows a bloke. Obviously there would be a small middleman fee involved, J.J."

"Don't worry." Scullen sighed. "You'll get your cut."

"There is just one small hole in this plot, my old son," the voice continued. "Unless I'm very much mistaken, you don't have the sparklers on your person, in which case some other person must have them. . . . What was his name again?"

"Cortesi!" Scullen spat out the name like it had soured his mouth just thinking of it.

"Yeah, that's right, Franco Cortesi. So how are you gonna get them from him?"

Scullen paused for a second and stared down at his huge dirty sneakers.

"I don't know yet, but I'm working on it."

"Might I suggest you work a little faster, 'cause I don't think old Franco boy will be hanging about once he knows you're back in his territory," the voice replied. "When are you coming down to see me?"

Scullen stared across the street at the bubble gum factory with the gaping wound in its side.

"I have another problem," he muttered into the mouthpiece.

The voice at the other end sighed. "What is it?"

"Have you ever heard the name Baresi?" Scullen's eyes narrowed as they scanned the street.

"Baresi? No, it doesn't ring a bell. Who is he?"

"I'm not sure who he is or where he's come from, but he's making a lot of moves up here in Lochrannoch."

"Oh yeah, looking for a bit of action, is he?" the voice smirked with excitement.

Scullen watched as a pile of bricks fell from the factory wall and smashed on the pavement.

"You could say that," he replied. "But I know one thing: If I'm going to take care of Cortesi, I'm going to have to take care of Baresi as well."

CHAPTER 13

Jake felt the sun stream through the classroom window. He brushed his hair away from his eyes and looked out at the playground as another group of kids went through the rigors of their phys ed class.

It felt good to have the sun on his face. The excitement of the past few weeks and the relentless promotion of the Big Baresi were taking its toll, but for this one isolated minute Jake allowed himself to drift off and forget about all that.

The noise of his classmates goofing off behind him as they waited for their teacher to arrive slowly dissolved in his ears. Not even the sight of a boy jumping off the filing cabinet, snagging his pants, and giving himself the world's worst wedgie could distract Jake from his semiconscious state; nor could the two people he hated most in the world, Dillon MacIlvoy and Buster Johnston, sneering at him from across the room. His former friend Eddie Tierney sat behind them, watching him over their shoulders.

Jake was just enjoying not thinking about Baresi, and it felt good.

"What do you think of my new badge, Jake?" The question stirred him back to reality.

Jake turned to see one of his classmates holding out the lapel of his blazer so he could get a good look at his new badge. It was a badge with the Baresi logo on it.

"Where did you get that?" asked Jake.

"The juniors are selling them in the toilets," the lad replied. "Only two pounds each."

Jake shook his head and looked back out the window; it seemed the Baresi logo had now become fashionable.

Outside on the playing field a teacher in a tracksuit was yelling at a small boy in an inflatable sumo suit. Jake couldn't hear what the teacher was shouting, but knew it probably involved the words "not the proper uniform for exercise class." A dressing down for dressing up.

Eventually the teacher pointed to a bench and the boy lumbered over to it, taking a seat beside the other five kids in sumo suits.

"OK, settle down, class, everyone get in your seats." Jake didn't recognize the voice. It wasn't his usual teacher, Mrs. MacDougal, with the hairy top lip.

"My name is Miss Primrose Peetling, and I will be your substitute English teacher for the next couple of weeks."

Miss Peetling was different from most of Jake's other teachers. For a start she didn't have wet patches under her arms or walk with a limp, and she had all her own teeth. Jake thought she looked quite nice in a plain sort of way; she was neither tall nor small but still had to look up to most of the boys. Her blonde hair was pulled back into a ponytail and her shirt was tucked into her long skirt.

"Mrs. MacDougal is unwell at the moment . . ."

"She cut herself shaving," mumbled an anonymous voice from the back, forcing a few hushed giggles from around the class. Miss Peetling waited for them to subside before continuing.

". . . and I know you will all wish her a speedy recovery. Now, today there will be no English lesson."

"Whoo-hoo!" The joyous shouts came from all around the classroom. Jake joined in.

"Instead, we have a special guest who wants to talk to you about a very important subject. Class, please say good morning to Officer Lewis Telford."

Oh, no! Jake screamed the words inside his head. *They're on to me.*

The door to the class opened and Officer Lewis Telford stood in the doorway. He was very tall. The tallest man Jake had ever seen, in fact, yet he didn't appear scary. It might have been because he was poker thin, or it might have been the way he tripped over the step, fell onto a desk, and sent Huffy, the class hamster, hurtling across the room in its cage.

Not the best of starts, Jake thought.

"Hello, boys and girls," said Officer Telford awkwardly as he picked himself up from the floor, "my name is Police Constable Lewis Telford. Well, actually, that isn't my name — it's just Lewis Telford — but I am a police constable."

The classroom remained silent and still.

Nervously the policeman cleared his throat. Primrose Peetling placed a reassuring hand on his arm. Officer Telford turned to her and smiled.

"Hello, Primrose," he said bashfully. "I mean Peetling . . . I, um, mean Miss Peetling."

He gazed at her for a long time before he finally realized he should be looking at the class instead and turned back to speak to them. "Today I would like to talk to you about the dangers of crime . . ."

Jake coughed and spluttered; every pair of eyes in the class turned and looked at him until he finally signaled he was OK. Officer Telford continued, ". . . in particular organized crime, and how it can swallow you up if you're not careful. Now, class, I'd like you all to help me conduct a short experiment. Hands up, anyone in here who knows a criminal."

Jake looked around the class. One by one a swarm of hands slowly raised in the air. "Excellent," commented the policeman, "you all know criminals. Well, obviously it's not excellent, but you know what I mean. I hope."

The hands dropped back down onto their desks.

"Now put your hands up if the criminal you know has gone to jail at some point or another."

A murmur broke out around the classroom as only a few hands rose upward.

"Oh, right." Officer Telford surveyed the class, more than a little shocked. "I don't suppose you're all thinking about the same person, are you? No, of course not, that was a silly question. The criminals you know must be pretty clever."

Miss Peetling coughed gently, a reminder to Officer Telford that he should just get on with his talk.

"Well, rest assured," he continued, "one day they will go to jail because a police officer like me will catch them. At least I hope I'll catch them. I haven't caught anyone yet. I'm quite new to this police game, you see; I used to be an accountant."

A ripple of giggles rose up from the back of the class and swelled forward.

"Crime does not pay!" he yelled triumphantly over the oncoming surf of snickers.

Instantly Jake's mind raced back to Cortesi's parting comment when he was leaving his office.

"Crime *does* pay," shouted Dillon MacIlvoy from the back of the class, as though he'd heard what was in Jake's head. "I know an armed robber and he's got three cars — and two of them are BMWs!"

"Yes, well, I'll admit sometimes crime does pay, and it can be quite lucrative. I suppose if you're really clever you won't get caught." Officer Telford drifted off as he spoke, as if he was actually contemplating a life of crime as another career change.

Miss Peetling looked on aghast as Officer Telford unwittingly encouraged a class of twelve-year-olds to a life on the wrong side of the law.

"What about the Big Baresi?" someone shouted.

Jake gripped his pencil so tightly that it snapped in his hands, making him jump.

"Ah, the Big Baresi," said Officer Telford. "We know all about the Big Baresi. Though when I say we know *all* about him, that's not strictly true; there are still some small details we need clarification on."

"Like what?" asked a girl near the front of the class. Jake looked on, wide-eyed.

"What he looks like, sounds like, where he lives, where he works, and who he works with."

"So," replied the girl, "you don't really know anything then?"

"Not a lot," conceded Officer Telford. "We do know that a number of crimes that have been committed recently have a lot to do with this Baresi person."

Jake listened intently in a mild state of panic.

Help, he thought. *What if he finds out I'm Baresi? Baresi's taken the credit for every beating and accident in the projects in the past week. I'll do time for this — the only twelve-year-old in the Barlinnie Big House!*

The classroom became a courtroom as he imagined himself answering for the crimes. His classmates became the jury as Jake Drake stood to enter his plea.

"Jake Drake, aka the Big Baresi," Judge Telford said, scowling, "you are accused of lobbing some nasty bloke down an elevator shaft. How do you plead?"

"Not guilty, Your Honor." Jake swallowed hard.

"That's a lie for a start," replied Judge Telford, "and what about nicking a truck full of knock-offs?"

"Not guilty, Your Honor."

Jake imagined his clothes ripping as an inflatable sumo suit he was wearing suddenly inflated and wedged him in the witness stand.

"I can't be bothered with this," growled Judge Telford. "The court finds you guilty." The wooden gavel smashed down, sealing Jake's fate, as he looked on in disbelief.

"Now for your sentence. Let's say ten years . . . no, wait, twenty years. Oh, blast it; the rest of your natural life behind bars. Take him down, and for goodness' sake, would somebody get him a haircut?"

"No!" screamed Jake. "I didn't mean for any of this to happen!"

"However, we are following some very positive lines of . . . pardon?"

Back in the classroom Officer Telford was interrupted in midramble by Jake's outburst.

"You didn't want any of what to happen?"

Jake turned to find his imaginary courtroom gone, and every pair of eyes in his classroom staring at him.

"I, um, I meant to say, ahem, I, ah . . ." Jake struggled to engage his brain.

"Nobody accused you of being the Big Baresi, my boy." Officer Telford looked a little bemused. "You can't be a leading player in the underworld; you're just a kid."

Jake felt his stomach drop down to where his butt should be, as Officer Telford's unwitting sympathy brought the entire class's gaze to his face. Dillon MacIlvoy smirked as Buster Johnston mouthed an obscenity across the room at Jake.

"Officer Telford, could we please just concentrate on the reason for your visit, and get back to the discussion?" said Miss Peetling.

"Yes, of course, Miss Peetling," replied the police officer, smiling at Jake. "You're not the man we're looking for. You don't fit his description at all."

Jake tried to smile back, but his shaken nerves pulled the corner of his mouth down to join his stomach and his butt.

"This Baresi fellow can't hide in the shadows forever," continued Officer Telford confidently. "We're closing the net and soon the only person left in it will be him!"

Jake's collar felt like a noose around his neck, and it was getting tighter and tighter and tighter.

CHAPTER 14

The long black cavalcade of cars rolled over the top of the hill, past the abandoned factories with their boarded-up windows and walls covered in graffiti, down the road toward Cortesi's graffiti-free garage at the bottom.

The midafternoon sun glistened off each car's gleaming paintwork but couldn't penetrate the blacked-out glass windows.

Sandwiched between two SUVs and surrounded by black BMWs was a vintage Mercedes-Benz limousine.

As the cars slowed near the entrance to the garage, the two rear doors on each SUV opened simultaneously. Shiny black shoes hung out of each door as the bodyguards inside waited for the cars to stop.

The second the wheels stopped turning, two men jumped from each vehicle, their hands ominously clutching something inside their black suit jackets as their eyes, concealed behind dark sunglasses, rapidly scanned the surroundings.

The driver and front passenger from the lead BMW got out and immediately strode inside the garage.

Then the doors on the car at the back of the cavalcade opened and another two hulking bodyguards appeared. They walked straight to the limousine that was still tucked between the two SUVs at the curb, and stood on either side of its back doors.

Everything was timed to perfection, every movement was synchronized.

Each bodyguard was like a clone of the other. Black suits, white shirts, black ties, obligatory sunglasses, and a suspicious bulge in their jackets.

The gentle hum of the Mercedes ceased as one of the guards emerged from inside the garage and nodded to his colleagues beside the limousine.

Instantly the limo door opened and the guards stepped closer, shielding whoever was getting out.

With a loud *thump,* the door slammed shut and the guards quickly walked toward the entrance of the garage, their enormous frames concealing the person behind them.

As they moved, the other bodyguards joined them and formed a protective circle, their eyes continuously scrutinizing everything around them.

Inside the garage, one of Franco Cortesi's mechanics looked on as the bank of bodyguards forming the human shield clumped toward him. Among the huge size-twelve shoes that formed the outer ring, he could see a pair of tiny size-five feet, moving twice as fast to keep up.

Calmly he picked up the telephone and dialed through to another office.

"Boss," he said. "Mickey Chang is here!"

Franco Cortesi puffed nervously on his cigar, a thick cloud of smoke hanging in the air above his chair.

He was doing his best to look cool and calm and collected, but the small beads of sweat trickling down the sides of his face told a different story.

Slowly he spun his leather recliner around to face his guest.

Mickey Chang was notorious throughout the south side of the city, where he held a knife to the criminal underbelly and controlled its every movement through fear and intimidation. Anyone who stepped on Chang's toes would most often find themselves staring down at a machete as it lopped their own toes off.

He didn't just have a hand in every crime that was committed, most often he'd have two arms, two legs, and a head as well.

He was big in robberies, big in extortion, and big in murder.

Yet tiny in person.

Chang sat down in the opposite chair. Cortesi stared across the desk at his pale forehead, barely visible above the edge of his desk. Pulling his chair closer, he leaned forward to get a better look at his terrifying guest.

Mickey Chang stared back at him.

His hair was pulled back to the left, slicked down and shiny. His warm brown eyes did a good job of masking his cold, calculating heart. For years Mickey had ruled the south side with his twin brother, Jimmy. They were exact opposites in every way. They thought differently, they fought differently, they even dressed differently. If Mickey wore a white suit with black shirt and tie, Jimmy wore a black suit with white shirt and tie. They looked like negative images of each other: Yin and Yang.

Until one day their bickering ended in bloodshed. Now there was only Yin.

"It is widiculous that we haven't met before." Cortesi eventually broke the silence. His high-pitched voice escaped through a fake smile, and smoke poured out between his teeth as if a grenade had just gone off in his mouth.

"I would like to say thank you for meeting with me. I know you are a vewy busy man."

Mickey sat in silence, staring back at Cortesi.

"Wecently I have encountered some pwoblems with my business. Pwoductivity is down, pwofits are down, and it's all thanks to one person — the Big Bawesi."

Cortesi leaned back in his chair and looked toward the ceiling.

"Well, I think he is 'big,'" he continued, "the coward has never shown his face."

"He sounds like a very clever man to me," replied Mickey, his voice barely raised above a whisper.

Cortesi sat straight up and stared at the forehead hardly visible above his desk.

"I've had associates fall down elevator shafts, my twuck full of merchandise was stolen just the other day, and my network of cwiminals is wunning scared. Whatever way you want to look at it, Bawesi is causing a lot of twouble for me . . ."

Cortesi sat back again and nodded across at the top of Mickey's head.

". . . and we hear he's going to cause twouble for you, too."

"You mean once he's disposed of you, I'm next on his list?"

Cortesi nodded. "I have it on good authwity that your tewwitory will be his next port of call. He wants total contwol."

"Is that right?" The voice rose over the desk from Mickey's forehead. "And I suppose you want me to help you out of this spot of bother? Well, what's in it for me?"

"I was thinking we could help each other get wid of Bawesi, and avoid any more twouble," answered Cortesi. "After all, we alweady have a working welationship in place. I stay out of your patch, and you stay out of mine. Bawesi will wuin that for us both."

"Give me a second," Mickey interrupted, standing up on his chair and running his fingers over his immaculate white tie. "I need to discuss this with my brother."

"Your bwother?" Cortesi asked, confused. "I thought your bwother, Jimmy, was dead?"

"Just because I killed him doesn't mean I can't still talk to him," replied Mickey very matter-of-factly. "It's not like we've fallen out over it."

Cortesi listened as Mickey whispered loudly and rolled his dark eyes to the ceiling. Half of what he said was in English and half in Chinese.

"Well, what does your bwother think you should do?" Cortesi couldn't quite believe he was asking the question.

"He thinks I should just walk away," replied Mickey Chang, sitting down again, "but I never do what he wants. I'll help you find this Baresi, and when we do, I'll help you dispose of him."

Cortesi puffed on his cigar and smiled.

"Tewiffic! I'm sure between us we'll find him and finish him quicker." Cortesi spun his cigar box around and slid it to the end of the desk. "Please join me in a cigar to cement our new working welationship."

A small hand reached over the desk and lifted a cigar from the box.

"What about John Joseph Scullen?" said Mickey, his voice floating through a cloud of cigar smoke.

Cortesi's smile dropped instantly.

"What about Scullen?" he asked cagily.

"What I'm asking is whether Scullen will distract you from finding Baresi." Mickey Chang's soft tone was unsettling. "I hear he got out of jail not long ago."

"Yes, I'm well aware of Scullen," answered Cortesi curtly. "He will not distwact me in any way. I haven't seen or heard fwom him since his welease. I doubt vewy much whether he would be silly enough to come back to Lochwannoch."

"I've heard lots of rumors that he is back in Lochrannoch already. I hear he is back for diamonds; some say it's over a million pounds' worth."

Cortesi puffed more quickly on his cigar, his eyes narrowing as he stared at the small forehead opposite him. A nervous tension hung in the air with the thick cigar smoke.

"I pwomise you that Scullen will not pose a pwoblem."

"Just out of interest, how did you manage to sell nearly three million dollars' worth of stolen jewels? The police must have been watching you."

"I asked you here to talk about Bawesi," replied Cortesi, "not my finances. Now, if we have nothing else to discuss wegarding Bawesi, then I have some work to be getting on with. . . ."

Mickey Chang immediately stood up, nodded politely to Cortesi, then jumped from his chair and walked toward the door.

"Wemember, if you find out anything about Bawesi just—"

"Baresi will be dead in a couple of days," the soft voice of Chang interrupted. "I don't care if I have to chop up every man, woman, and child to find him. I will do it!"

The door slammed shut and Cortesi was alone in his office. He let out a relieved sigh and picked up another cigar.

Rings of smoke puffed into the air as Cortesi quickly ran over the conversation in his mind. He picked up the telephone and dialed through to the garage.

"Send those two idiots in here right now!" he barked down the line.

Outside on the pavement, Cortesi's own Tweedle-Dumb and Tweedle-Dumber stood looking through a small opening in the limousine window.

"You have to be clever now, boys," Mickey Chang reminded them from the darkness inside the car. "Remember what we've agreed. Once I kill Baresi, I'm coming after Cortesi, so you must decide who you want to work for."

Tweedle-Dumb looked at his colleague and swallowed hard.

"Stick to the plan, keep it simple. All you have to do is just make a call and let me do the rest."

Dumb and Dumber nodded thoughtfully.

"Find out where Cortesi is keeping the diamonds, and then pick up the phone."

"OK, we know what to do," said Tweedle-Dumb, nervously combing his mustache with his fingers.

"If he is suspicious," continued Mickey Chang, "he'll think about moving the jewels somewhere different, just to be on the safe side. All you have to do is make that call."

The window was wound up and the cars slowly pulled away.

Both men watched the cavalcade as it made its way back up the hill, then dropped over the other side and out of sight.

"Where the heck have you two clowns been?" screamed Cortesi. "I buzzed for you a couple of minutes ago."

Tweedle-Dumb closed the door behind him and quickly joined his colleague in the middle of the office floor.

"Were you two fwolicking with those Dubble girls again?"

"No, Boss, we were just . . . ah . . . err . . ." Tweedle-Dumber couldn't find the words.

"Oh, shut up and listen!" Cortesi shouted. "I'm going to be moving something soon and it's

THE ICE CREAM CON

vewy valuable. I want it well pwotected. I want some extwa muscle bwought in."

Dumb and Dumber looked at each other knowingly.

"Well, get on with it, you pair of patsies."

"Sure, Boss," the taller of the goons replied, "we'll just make a call."

CHAPTER 15

Jake felt a murderous rage build inside him.

Shards of broken glass cracked under his feet as he walked around his garage.

Underneath his overturned desk lay a picture of his parents, the last one to be taken before their accident. The frame was broken in two.

Jake stopped in the center of the space and looked around.

His couch lay on its back; the cushions had been torn and thrown across the place, spilling their insides all over the floor. Pictures and posters had been smashed and torn; anything breakable was broken into pieces. The Beast lay under a table. Whoever had ransacked Jake's place had also used his bat to good effect.

"We've looked around, but whoever did it is long gone." Aidan was out of breath as he and Harvey slipped under the garage door. The bottom left corner turned out and upward, the metal bent completely out of shape.

Someone or something very strong had forced its way into the garage.

"Do you think whoever did this, Jake, knows that you're the Big Baresi?" Harvey tried to settle his breathing as he spoke.

"I don't know," Jake mumbled back, picking up his overturned chair and taking a seat.

"It was probably just an opportunist thief," said Aidan, "some career criminal from the projects."

"Well, today was his lucky day." Jake sighed, kicking a long metal container across the floor. It was empty except for a few loose coins.

"Dude!" exclaimed Harvey. "Did they get all the money?"

"Every penny," replied Jake, his head slumped against the side of the chair. "We've lost just over twenty grand in cash."

Aidan whistled through his teeth as he surveyed the damage inside the garage.

"Look on the bright side, dude," said Harvey. "At least it wasn't our money. When you think about it, someone has stolen our stolen money, which we stole off of someone else who had stolen it."

Jake tried to absorb Harvey's reasoning before shaking it out of his head.

"We were going to do some good with it," Jake answered back.

"Oh yeah, like what?" Aidan asked.

"I don't know; maybe use it to get the community center reopened or something. Give us all somewhere to go at night, like we used to."

Aidan smirked a smirk that told Jake he didn't believe him.

"What if it wasn't an opportunist thief?" Harvey interjected. "What if the person who did this knew you had all that cash hidden in here?"

"That's crazy," Jake replied. "The only people who knew about the money was us three and—"

"Me!" shouted Sofia as she stooped under the door. "And I didn't steal it, but I know who did!"

Jake slowly raised himself out of his chair.

"How do you know?" he asked.

Sofia brushed her hair away from her face and tucked it behind her ears.

"I was passing by here about an hour ago and I saw him leave the garage."

"Who?" asked Aidan.

"I don't know," Sofia replied. "I didn't recognize him."

"What use is that?" Aidan raised his voice in disbelief.

"I didn't recognize him," Sofia yelled back, "so I followed him."

"Where did he go?" asked Jake, pacing up and down the garage floor.

"I followed him across to the towers . . ."

"So he lives in one of those apartments!" Jake interrupted her.

"No," she retorted, "he walked straight past them across to your tenement block."

"He's one of your neighbors, Jake!" Harvey couldn't believe his ears.

"No," said Sofia, "he walked straight past the tenements out to the edge of the projects, to the new buildings the city council has built near the main road."

"Where did he go then?" asked Jake impatiently.

"Right into apartment number ninety-three."

"Good!" Jake stopped pacing and lifted his desk onto its legs. "What did he look like?"

Sofia stopped smiling.

"He was huge, Jake, taller than six feet, and he must have weighed about two fifty. His head is completely shaven, like a skinhead's, and he has a really nasty look in his eyes."

Jake looked at his friends' faces. It was clear they didn't relish the idea of confronting the robber in person.

"I asked one of his neighbors his name," Sofia continued. "He told me it was Scullen, John Joseph Scullen."

Jake slumped down into his chair.

"But that's not all; the neighbor told me he just got out of jail, for armed robbery."

"Oh, it's getting better all the time," said Aidan sarcastically. "Well, we can kiss bye-bye to the money. There's no way we're going to get it back."

"What are we going to do, Jake?" Sofia asked.

Jake leaned forward.

"I'll tell you what we're going to do," he replied defiantly. "We *are* going to get the money back."

Aidan, Harvey, and Sofia looked at one another out of the corners of their eyes.

"You can count me out," said Aidan.

"Me, too," Harvey joined him.

"And me," Sofia concurred.

"All right, then," Jake continued, "I'll just have to visit Mr. Scullen on my own!"

CHAPTER 16

There were four hundred and sixteen roof tiles above apartment number ninety-three.

Seven of which were loose.

Jake looked at his watch. The time was quarter past nine, and he should have been in his first class fifteen minutes ago.

Instead Jake lay on the cold wet mound across from John Joseph Scullen's place and tried his best to stay focused, which was hard, since he'd lain there for nearly two hours.

In that time he'd checked his watch forty-seven times, yawned twelve times, picked his nose twice, and was still waiting to break wind for the first time that day.

He'd counted the roof tiles, sent three text messages, and laughed at the mailman who'd slipped on some dog poo.

Earlier Jake had enjoyed the thought of staking out Scullen's apartment, but the reality turned from excitement to boredom as the monotony of staring at two windows and a door kicked in.

"Come on," Jake said out loud. "Get out of bed, you lazy—"

Just then the handle to Scullen's door swung downward and a very tall, bald-headed man appeared in the doorway. His frame almost equaled the door's as he stepped out and slammed it shut behind him.

Jake could feel his heart beating faster as he watched Scullen leave his apartment and walk along the landing, past the other doors, to the stairs at the end.

Bzzzz, bzzzz. Bzzzz, bzzzz.

Jake's cell phone started to vibrate in his pocket. Quickly he pulled it out and saw Harvey's number on the screen.

"What is it, Harvey? I'm busy," he answered.

"I know, dude, I can see you."

"Where are you?"

"To your left, behind the blue van."

Jake looked across to the parking lot and saw Harvey standing behind the van, his face half hidden by his balaclava.

"Take off the headgear!" Jake muffled his own yell.

"Why?"

"Because it's too early in the morning to look like a bank robber. You'll attract attention."

Harvey rolled up the ski mask until it sat like a hat on top of his head.

"Dude, are you really going to break into his pad?"

"Of course," Jake replied. "He broke into my garage."

John Joseph Scullen emerged from the shadows of the ground-floor stairwell. The cold morning air bit at his face as he pulled up the collar of his denim jacket.

"Well, I'm here for you, Jake," said Harvey as he watched Scullen pass behind him and head down toward the main road. "I've got your back."

"Thanks, bro," Jake replied. "Let me know if he is coming back, and remember, try and look inconspicuous."

"No problem, dude."

"You don't know what that means, do you?" Jake sighed.

"Nope."

"Just try not to look out of place, try to look normal."

Jake lifted himself from the wet grass and started across the lot toward the corner stairwell. His hands began to sweat as he drew closer to the stairs. He could hear his own heart beating in his ears. The truth was, Jake himself couldn't quite believe what he was about to do, but knew he had to do it if he wanted to get the money back.

Quickly he climbed the stairs two at a time, the sound of his footsteps echoing as he ran. The daylight streamed down the last flight as Jake quickly ascended and emerged out onto the landing of the fourth floor, the top floor.

His heavy breathing made small plumes of cold air appear before his face.

"C'mon, Jake," he said to himself. "You can do this."

Door after door blurred past as Jake ran along the landing toward number ninety-three at the end.

He looked down to the parking lot. Occasionally he would catch a glimpse of Harvey rolling between parked cars like a thigh-high special ops agent.

As he reached the blue door of Scullen's apartment, he stopped and wiped the sweat from his forehead.

Boom-boom, boom-boom, boom-boom—his heart pounded in his ears.

Jake knelt down and looked at the lock on the door.

"Just try the handle!" Harvey's scream echoed all around the apartment complex.

"Shut up!" Jake shouted back in the loudest whisper he could muster.

Idiot! he thought to himself as he flapped his arms wildly toward Harvey, not in any particular motion but out of pure frustration.

Jake turned back to the door.

"Just try the handle!" He spat out Harvey's words in disbelief. "As if . . ."

Jake turned the handle and the door of the apartment clicked open.

"Told you!" The shout echoed all over the parking lot once again.

Jake quickly slipped inside and closed the door behind him.

The long hallway was dimly lit, with three doors on one side and one slightly ajar straight ahead.

Through the gap he could see what looked like the corner of an armchair and guessed that must be the den.

Slowly Jake made his way down the hall; he could feel cold sweat running down his back. His hands trembled with nerves as he reached the first door.

Boom-boom, boom-boom, boom-boom—his heart continued to race as he raised his hand and pushed the door.

It slid open with a loud creak. As daylight poured through the door into the hallway, Jake stepped inside. Underneath the bare window was a long bath; above it on a thin rope hung wet clothes. Against the wall was a sink and a toilet.

The bathroom was not how Jake had imagined it would be. There were no blood smatterings rising up the wall, no body limbs lying in the bathtub, no sharp knives in sight. Just a packet of disposable razors and some roll-on deodorant lying beside the sink.

Jake pulled the door closed behind him and continued down the hallway.

Boom-boom, boom-boom, boom-boom.

The second door didn't open as easily as the first. The carpet was thicker and so Jake had to push harder. The door thumped to a stop before it was fully open.

Jake peered around the door and saw a rowing machine lying just behind it. Two well-ironed shirts lay on a freshly made-up bed.

Jake could feel the nerves fluttering in the pit of his stomach as he stepped over the rowing machine and crouched down beside the bed.

He lifted up the quilt and bedsheets, took a firm grip of the mattress, and heaved it up. All that was underneath was wooden support slats; no cash.

The mattress thumped down as Jake dropped it and walked toward the closet. His hands were moist with sweat as he pulled open the double doors.

Four shirts and a sweater hung from a rail, beside lots of empty hangers.

In between picking his nose and counting roof tiles, Jake had thought about what he'd do once inside the apartment. He'd imagined himself rummaging through all the clothes to find the money, but instead stood staring into the almost empty closet of a man fresh out of jail.

Equally, his chest of drawers was not only empty of cash but empty of clothes as well.

The bedroom door swished closed as Jake pulled it behind him and continued with the search.

Boom-boom, boom-boom, boom-boom.

The last door didn't have a handle that turned, but one designed to be pulled open.

Jake wiped his palm against his jeans and took hold of it: With a loud pop the door pinged open and something jumped on him from the darkness.

Jake screamed and fell back, punching and kicking until it landed beside him on the hall carpet. Quickly he rolled away onto his knees and spun around to see what it was.

A long kitchen mop lay harmlessly beside him.

Jake sighed with relief and, after taking a few seconds to compose himself, returned the mop to the hall closet. His eyes strained as he tried to see what else was hidden in the darkness.

An old metal bucket lay near his feet on the floor, and a modern vacuum cleaner stood behind it, its power cord coiled neatly at the side.

Jake pushed the door closed and turned toward the den.

Boom-boom, boom-boom, boom-boom. The pounding of his heart played like drums in his ears.

Jake stepped into the den.

A brown leather couch lined a long wall broken near the end with another doorway. Jake presumed it was the door to the kitchen.

A glass coffee table stood in the center of the floor, in front of a white fireplace. Car magazines were piled neatly on top of it. A silver wide-screen TV perched on its metallic stand in the corner, and underneath sat a matching silver DVD player.

The entire apartment was very different from what Jake had expected.

He had imagined blood and guts and severed limbs, and chains and bats and guns, and dirt and grime and filth stretching from one corner of the place to the next.

But he'd never expected cleanliness, or tidiness, or tastefulness.

Jake quickly walked to the couch and flipped up the seat cushions. No money.

He pushed his hands down the back. Again, no money.

He lifted the front of the couch off the floor and with his head on the carpet peered underneath. Still no money.

"Where the heck is it?" he muttered out loud.

He picked himself up from the carpet and marched into the kitchen.

Cabinet doors swung open in quick succession as Jake moved from one to the next. Drawers slammed shut as his search for the stolen twenty thousand pounds gathered pace, but still gave him nothing.

"Come on!" he shouted as he climbed onto the countertops and ran his hands along the top of the cabinets.

With a thud he landed back in the middle of the floor. His breathing was heavy as he looked around the kitchen, muttering under his breath.

"Where did you hide it?" he mumbled. "Where?"

Jake turned slowly and looked at a tall white fridge pushed back against the far wall.

"Gotcha!" he whispered, smiling, and paced the floor toward it.

Boom-boom, boom-boom, boom-boom.

He dried the sweat from his palms on the front of his jeans.

Boom-boom, boom-boom, boom-boom.

His hand grabbed the handle.

Bzzzz, bzzzz.

The sound of his mobile made him jolt. He pulled the phone from his pocket.

Harvey Mobile flashed on the screen.

"What is it?" he snapped.

"Dude, you've got to get out of there now! There are two men heading straight for the place!"

Jake froze to the spot. A cold sensation ran through his whole body, as though his blood had turned to ice.

"Is it Scullen?"

"No," Harvey replied anxiously. "I don't know who they are—just get out now!"

Jake sprinted out of the kitchen into the den.

Boom-boom, boom-boom, boom-boom.

Through the den and into the hallway.

Boom-boom, boom-boom, boom-boom.

He stopped suddenly.

Two shadows appeared through the window of the front door at the end of the hall.

The door trembled as one of the men banged loudly on it with his fist.

Boom-boom, boom-boom, boom-boom—his heart was ready to burst from his chest.

Jake stood in the hallway, not knowing what to do. The handle turned downward.

Daylight appeared on the carpet as the door slowly opened.

A pair of brown leather shoes stepped inside.

"There's nobody here," the man said, pushing the door wide and stepping into the empty hallway.

Jake tried to calm his breathing inside the hall closet. Panic poured through his veins as he watched the men's shadows on the wall through a gap in the open door.

"Oh, Big Baresi!" the voice sung mockingly.

Jake recoiled to the back of the closet with shock.

"Come on in," a second voice said.

Jake watched the daylight disappear from the carpet as the front door clicked shut.

Who the heck are they? the words screamed inside his head. *How do they know I'm Baresi?*

"Why didn't he lock the door?" the first voice asked, getting closer to Jake.

"Why should he?" the other voice answered. "If you were a robber, would you break into the Big Baresi's house?"

"Definitely not. It's a good job we're coppers then, eh?"

"Police!" The word escaped Jake's mouth before he could stop it.

The men continued past the closet door. Jake stole a glimpse through the crack as the slender frame of Officer Surpress slipped into the den, followed quickly by the pudgy posterior of Chief Stone.

"You still think Scullen is Baresi?" Surpress asked.

Jake pressed his ear to the wall and listened to the muffled conversation.

"Don't you?" Stone replied.

"I suppose," Surpress conceded. "He didn't come back to Lochrannoch for nothing."

The words tumbled in Jake's head as he tried to absorb them.

Scullen is Baresi? He turned the theory over in his mind; it was one he wasn't expecting.

"We know what he came back for," Stone continued.

Jake could hear furniture being moved around.

"He came back for Cortesi's loot; three million dollars in diamonds."

Jake mouthed the amount to himself, but it didn't make any sense.

"Well, he's dicing with death," Surpress replied. "If what we hear is true, Baresi doesn't just have Cortesi to contend with now, he's got Mickey Chang as well."

Who on earth is Mickey Chang? thought Jake.

"That's an unholy alliance if ever I heard one," said Stone. "Once Chang kills Baresi, he'll go after Cortesi. He'll probably wait until he knows where Cortesi is hiding the ice."

Kills Baresi! The words sounded in Jake's ears like a warning.

"Mickey Chang must have a snitch inside Cortesi's camp, probably those two idiots he calls Tweedle-Dumb and Dumber."

"The two clowns who are dating the Dubble girls?" Surpress asked.

"Yeah, the same guys," Stone replied, "and the same Dubble twins who work for Cortesi — the man who got their parents jailed a few years back. I helped set them up for a credit-card scam Cortesi was running. They were just a couple of small-timers."

"I wonder what would happen if the girls ever found *that* out," Surpress snorted.

Chang is double-crossing Cortesi? Dumb and Dumber are working with Chang? Cortesi double-crossed the Dubble Ds' parents? Jake's head spun as he tried to take it all in.

And everybody's trying to kill the Big Baresi!

Jake swallowed hard and wiped the sweat from his forehead. For the first time since he'd created the Big Baresi, he felt like he was in way over his head.

"Really, when you think about it, it all fits together nicely for us."

Jake could hear the smirk in Stone's voice.

"When Chang kills Baresi and Cortesi, we'll get rid of Mickey Chang and split the diamonds."

The den door opened suddenly. Jake watched through the gap as Officer Surpress stood in the doorway, pondering his thoughts.

"Yeah, you're right," he said over his shoulder, his hand grabbing the knob of the hall closet door. "I think we're close to getting out of this cesspit city."

Jake stopped breathing.

"Have you found anything yet?" Stone shouted from the other room.

"Not yet," Surpress replied, his hand still on the doorknob. "No calling cards, no sumo suits, nothing."

Jake closed his eyes.

"Let's get out of here before Scullen gets back."

Jake opened one eye as Surpress let go of the doorknob and disappeared back up the hallway and out of view.

"You know what?" said Stone, following his colleague. "I think today we got closer to the Big Baresi than anyone ever has."

The front door slammed shut and Jake let out a sigh of relief. His back slid down the wall as he slumped to the ground, breathing heavily. His hands started trembling as he relived how close he'd come to being caught.

He waited a few minutes to regain his composure before finally clambering to his feet. Quietly he pushed the closet door open and stepped into the hallway. His head rested against the door as it clicked shut, and he steadied his breathing.

"Relax," he said out loud. "You got away with it."

Jake turned toward the front door, but before he could take another step his heart stopped.

John Joseph Scullen stood in the center of the hallway, his nostrils flared with anger and his teeth clenched with fury as he stood staring at Jake.

Daylight poured through the open front door behind him.

"What the hell are you doing in my apartment?" he demanded, pacing angrily toward Jake.

Fear cemented Jake to the spot. He tried to reply but couldn't find the words.

"You stinking little thief!" Scullen spat the words as he grabbed hold of Jake.

"You're the thief!" Jake shouted back. "You broke into my garage."

"I what?" Scullen shook his head. "You've got the nerve to stand in my apartment and call *me* a thief?"

"What did you do with the money?" Fear was replaced by resolve as Jake went toe to toe with a six-foot-four-inch madman.

"What money?" Scullen replied, towering over Jake.

"The money you stole from my garage yesterday, and don't try to deny it, because my friend saw you."

"I'm not denying I was in your garage yesterday . . ."

"Good," Jake interrupted, "because I hate liars!"

". . . but I didn't steal your money. I saw two kids run out of your garage as I was passing. Your door was all busted so I checked inside to make sure everything was OK. It wasn't; they'd trashed the place. Then I left."

"Do you expect me to believe that?" shouted Jake. "You're a convicted criminal!"

Scullen stood up straight and took a deep breath. He looked almost offended by Jake's last remark.

"Maybe so," Scullen replied, "but right now you're the one who's in the wrong apartment."

Suddenly Jake was well aware that Scullen's fist was nearly the same size as his own head.

"All right, then." Jake swallowed. "What did these kids look like?"

"One was tall with blond hair and braces, the other one was chubby."

"I should have known." Jake sighed. "Dillon MacIlvoy and Buster Johnston, the Numb Nuts."

Scullen let go of Jake's arm and stepped to the side.

"I didn't come back here to rob a young boy of his pocket money," he said to Jake. "Now get out of here. You're lucky I haven't called the police."

"The police!" Jake replied. "They were just—" Jake stopped before he said too much.

"They were what?" Scullen asked suspiciously.

"Nothing," mumbled Jake as he squeezed past Scullen and walked toward the open door.

With every step he steeled himself for a punch to the back of the head.

It didn't arrive.

As Jake stepped from the apartment, the cold air was like a calming blanket that draped over him and soothed his palpitating heart back to a steady rhythm.

The door slammed hard at his heels, shaking the windows and giving Jake one last fright before he knew he was safe.

Bzzzz, bzzzz.

"Hello, Harvey," said Jake without checking the screen.

"Dude, are you all right?" Harvey stood looking up from the parking lot.

"I'm fine," Jake replied, still shaken.

"Did you get the money back?"

"No. He doesn't have it. It was the Numb Nuts who stole it."

"We'll get it back, dude."

Jake sighed, his mind still far away from the conversation his mouth was having.

"Forget the money, Harvey," he said. "We're in trouble. Big trouble."

"What kind of trouble?"

"They're coming after Baresi."

"Who is?"

"Everybody." Jake's voice began to tremble. "If I don't think of something fast, I'm a dead man."

CHAPTER 17

"You have to kill Baresi."

Aidan's words hit Jake like a punch in the stomach, very nearly winding him.

"Don't be so stupid, Aidan," he replied. "I can't kill him."

The daylight was fading fast over the park where Jake had gathered his friends. It was deserted now: The mothers and toddlers, and the joggers, had headed off before the light diminished completely and the lowlifes came to claim the park for their evening activities. They loitered by the swings, flanked on three sides by large hedgerows.

Aidan and Sofia listened in silence, in disbelief, and in fear as Jake recounted that day's earlier breaking-and-entering incident at Scullen's place.

Harvey had already heard the cops' comments from Jake, but couldn't help gasping with his friends at the dramatic moments in the tale. Even though he was wearing a sumo suit and playing on a swing at the time.

"Jake, I don't think you understand how much danger you're in," said Aidan calmly. "Cortesi wants Baresi dead, Mickey Chang wants Baresi dead, and the police want Baresi dead. If you don't find a way to kill Baresi now, they'll soon find out that you're Baresi, and you'll be dead!"

Jake took a deep breath and gazed across the park. As much as he hated the thought, he knew Aidan was right.

"I can't kill Baresi," he replied, shaking his head.

"Why not, Jake?" asked Sofia. "It's not like he's a real person."

"He is to me."

"Jake, listen," said Aidan pleadingly. "There are strange men all over the projects asking questions about Baresi, and the flyers, and especially the frickin' sumo suits. Jake, it's Chang's people, and they're closing in."

Just then they felt a faint vibration beneath their feet and a distant engine whine grew louder as something approached them from behind a line of high hedges.

"What on earth is that?" Sofia asked, moving back behind Jake.

"Hang on, I'll take a look!" Harvey shouted, whizzing upward on the swing.

As it rose, Harvey craned his neck to see over the hedges, until gravity took its toll and he swept back down again.

"Well, what did you see?" shouted Jake.

"Nothing," Harvey replied, scuffing his feet furiously to try and bring himself to a stop.

The trembling grew stronger and the sound got louder as whatever it was thundered toward them.

The hedges suddenly split and tore as two large, high-powered four-wheelers burst through the undergrowth, straight toward them.

"Yee-hah!" screamed Dillon MacIlvoy as he skidded his ATV to a stop just in front of Jake.

"It's the Numb Nuts!" shouted Aidan angrily.

Buster Johnston weaved through the swing frames and stopped his four-wheeler just behind his friend.

"How do you like my new ride, Drake?" MacIlvoy sneered. "It's brand-new, straight out of the box."

"How did you . . . uh . . . pay for that, Mr. MacIlvoy?" said Buster, like a bad actor trying hard to remember his lines.

"Well, Mr. Johnston, I paid for it with cash, no questions asked," Dillon replied, not taking his eyes off Jake.

"And where did you . . . um . . . get the cash?" Buster continued obediently.

"I swiped it from a jerk-off named Jake," MacIlvoy sneered. "He won't be feeling too grand right now. In fact he won't be feeling twenty grand."

Jake clenched his fists and flew at Dillon, but before he reached him MacIlvoy pulled back on the throttle and his ATV sped away, kicking grass and dirt into the air behind its fat tires.

Jake watched them zigzag across the park, laughing and hollering as they went, until they disappeared out of sight.

"There's another reason to get rid of Baresi," said Sofia quietly. "It won't take long before people start asking them questions about those. When they tell them they stole twenty thousand pounds from your garage, Jake, everything will be traced back to you."

Jake sighed and turned to his friends. Harvey was still trying to unwedge his sumo suit from the swing, but not having much luck.

"I'm not killing Baresi," Jake mumbled. "I've got an idea how we can get out of this mess, I just need more time to put the final pieces of my plan together."

"There is no *we,* Jake." Aidan looked down at his feet as he spoke. "We said right from the start that if anyone came calling, *you* were the Big Baresi. Well, people are coming calling."

Jake looked for support from Sofia and Harvey, but their eyes were on the ground with Aidan's.

"I can't kill him," pleaded Jake. "I can't kill Baresi; he's done a lot of good."

"Not everything he's done, dude, has been good," said Harvey, pulling at his sumo suit.

"If you can't kill him, Jake, we can't be around you right now." Aidan's words ripped through Jake's heart like bullets. "It's just too dangerous."

"Well, if that's the way it's got to be, then that's the way it's got to be."

Jake turned away from his friends and headed toward the projects. With every lonely step he took he prayed that one of his friends might shout his name, tell him it was OK, tell him they were all still a team.

All he heard was silence.

As he reached the end of the park, he looked back. Aidan and Sofia were busy trying to free Harvey from the swing.

When eventually they managed to pop him out, he sailed through the air and bounced around the ground in the suit, rolling from side to side until they helped him back to his feet.

"That's it!" shouted Jake. In an instant his dejection became exhilaration and he laughed out loud. "That's the final piece of the puzzle, Jakey boy. You're a freakin' genius! Now let's set this plan in motion."

CHAPTER 18

The pain comparisons ran through Jake's head in that instant of impact.

It was worse than the time Harvey handed him the electric eggbeater instead of the hair dryer.

It was way worse than the time Aidan placed a mousetrap in his sour-cream-and-onion chips.

And even though he couldn't remember it, Jake knew the time his grandmother absentmindedly rubbed curry powder on his diaper rash was nowhere near as bad.

No, thought Jake, *there is no pain assessment in existence that can accurately describe the excruciating please-God-end-it-now torture of being kicked in the goolies by a Dubble twin.*

It wasn't the speed at which Demi Dubble could move her mammoth leg that astounded Jake the most, but the accuracy with which her leg always found its target, like a laser-guided Caterpillar boot, locked onto Jake's knackers.

"Here we go again," he said to himself as the pain buckled his legs and his face hit the wet grass outside the Dubbles' ground-floor apartment.

"What do you make of him, Desiree?" Demi asked her oversized sibling in disbelief. "Interrupting our dinnertime with a mouthful of lies!"

"It's not lies," wheezed Jake, a thin layer of dirt clinging to the side of his face.

"You're a lying wee turd," shouted Desiree. At least that's what Jake thought she said, though he did have to decipher it through a mouthful of cooked chicken.

"Why would I make it up?" he asked them. By now the pain had started to dissolve into a tingling sensation in the pit of his stomach. "What good would that do?"

"You're always up to something, Jake Drake!" Demi snorted. "And I want to know what it is. Who told you it was Cortesi that ratted out our mum and dad?"

Jake gingerly got to his feet, like a weary boxer who'd just been counted out.

"I overheard two cops talking about it the other day."

Desiree dropped a gnawed chicken leg into a paper bucket and picked out another with the meat still on the bone.

"What two cops?" she barked. "What were their names?"

Jake was doubled over, still trying to coax some normality back to his nether regions.

"I don't know their names," he replied. "One was a tall skinny guy with dark hair, and the other was a little fat guy with gray hair."

Demi looked at Desiree knowingly.

"If you don't believe me," Jake continued, "go visit your parents; ask them if they think it could have been Cortesi."

"It could have been anyone that set them up." A half-chewed piece of chicken rolled around Desiree's mouth as she spoke. "There's no way of knowing for sure. So the question is — do we believe *you*?"

"That's true," Jake conceded, "but ask yourselves, *who* out of everyone you know has a special relationship with the police? And what would I get from spreading lies about Cortesi — apart from two broken legs?"

"You've never liked us, Jake," said Demi Dubble, "so why are you trying to help us?"

"I don't like you now, but I need your help."

"With what?" asked Desiree.

"I'll tell you once I can trust you, once I know you believe me about Cortesi."

Desiree looked suspicious.

"Fair enough, we'll ask our mum and dad, see if they think you might be telling the truth. But if they say it's a load of rubbish, we're coming after you, Jake!"

The mere thought made Jake's hands clutch protectively over his privates.

"Sorry for interrupting your dinnertime, ladies," he said apologetically. "I should have realized, it *is* almost eleven a.m."

"Are you being sarcastic?" asked Demi angrily.

"Sarcastic," said Jake to Desiree, "means sneering, jesting, or mocking a situation, a person, or a thing."

"Don't be so condescending, Jake!" Demi shouted angrily. "Desiree knows what it means."

Jake turned back to Desiree, he couldn't help himself.

"Condescending," he said, "means to display a superior attitude, to talk down to someone like I am now, or to belittle. Do you know what belittle means, Desiree?"

Desiree lifted her confused head from inside the bucket and turned to her sister, a piece of greasy chicken skin hanging from her bottom lip.

"Of course she knows what it means." Demi laughed. "Desiree, give Jake the definition."

Desiree spun around quickly, and before Jake could react, booted him three times in the goolies, in rapid succession.

"That is what it means," sneered Desiree.

Jake stared down between his legs, like he was on some sort of time delay, still trying to absorb the surprise of the attack. He'd known it was coming, but the speed was incredible.

"What do you know?" he said, lifting his head and smiling. "No pain. I didn't feel a thing. Thank you for your time, ladies, I must be on my way."

Jake turned and fell face-first into some hedges behind him. His legs stuck out from the bottom of the shrubs, trembling violently.

"I can't believe you did that!" Demi said to her sister. "That was really rotten."

"What?" replied Desiree.

"You ate all the chicken."

CHAPTER 19

Jake let his mind drift as the endless stream of headlights sped beneath him. The sound of tractor trailers and vans and cars mixed together in a thunderous rush-hour concoction as the evening commuters headed home on the packed stretch of highway.

It had taken Jake only ten minutes to walk from the center of Lochrannoch, past the newly demolished apartment buildings, through the strip mall with its boarded-up windows, and over the grass hill specially made to smother the noise from the busy highway, yet to him it felt like his projects were a whole world away.

As Jake stood on the walkway that passed over the traffic, he wondered whether *he* would show up.

Jake still had his cell number saved in his own phone. It had been over a year since he'd called the number, since he'd been betrayed.

In that time he'd gone from detesting him to merely hating him. But now he needed him.

Jake wasn't even sure if he'd received the text he'd sent him earlier that afternoon, since no reply had come back.

Jake looked at his watch; it was almost half past eight, and he was nearly thirty minutes late.

"Never mind, Jake." He sighed to himself. "You'll just have to think of another way of getting your hands on them."

He lifted his head and breathed in the night air.

"Jake!"

The voice startled him. Jake turned around.

Eddie Tierney stood in the center of the overpass, his hands inside a blue sports jacket. He stood alone; his usual friends, Dillon MacIlvoy and Buster Johnston, were nowhere to be seen.

"I didn't think you were going to show up," said Jake.

"I wasn't," Eddie replied.

"So why did you?"

Eddie went to answer but stopped short of saying anything.

"Don't think I'm here because I feel I owe you something," he eventually responded, stubbornly.

"I don't," said Jake. "I'm glad you showed up, anyway."

"What do you want, Jake? What's this about?" Eddie seemed uneasy.

"You look nervous, Eddie. Are you scared Dillon and Buster might be out for a romantic stroll together and see you talking to me?"

"You said you needed to talk; get on with it or I'm gone."

Jake thought twice about replying. It pained him to ask Eddie for help after all he'd done, but he knew it was the easiest way.

"I'm in trouble, serious trouble. I need you to help me get out of it. I need you to be my friend again."

Eddie stared impassively at Jake, without reply. It felt like forever to Jake before he spoke.

"What have you done now?" He smiled.

"How long have you got?" Jake smiled back.

Eddie laughed. "Long enough, bud. Now tell me what's going on."

CHAPTER 20

Jake swept the last of the broken glass into the dustpan.

It had taken him almost three hours of picking up furniture, rehanging pictures, and sweeping up debris to get his storage garage back to something resembling normality.

It shouldn't have taken him so long, but his mind wasn't really on the task at hand, he just couldn't stop thinking about Aidan, and Harvey, and Sofia.

He realized that since he had been friends with them, he hadn't felt the same sickening, empty feeling he'd felt for so long after his parents died.

But he was experiencing it again now.

Jake slumped into his chair; the weight of his worries pulled his head facedown onto the desk. After every emotion he'd experienced since creating the Big Baresi—fear, excitement, dread, exhilaration, panic, and even hopelessness—it was the one he hadn't expected that sent a tear down his cheek.

Loneliness.

The events of the past few weeks flicked rapidly through his mind, like an old film playing at the wrong speed.

Images of overweight bullies and huge balding gangsters with speech impediments flashed before his eyes. He could see his friends, laughing as they stuck flyers to walls, screaming as Jake drove them through the bubble gum factory, despairing as they parted ways in the park.

"You really know how to mess things up big time." Jake sighed to himself. "Your stupid ideas have lost you the only real friends you've ever had."

"Hey, Baresi, this plan of yours had better be a good one."

The voice startled Jake upright.

Aidan stood in the middle of the room. Harvey and Sofia were just behind.

"Dude, have you been crying?" asked Harvey.

Jake quickly rubbed his hand across his cheek.

"Uh, no . . . I must have . . . um, fallen asleep," replied Jake, not making eye contact. "What are you doing back here? I thought you couldn't be around me just now."

"We started this together," Aidan replied, "so we'll finish it together. Besides, you'll never be able to take them all on, not on your own."

Jake smiled, a feeling of warm relief swelled inside him, he wanted to say something gushy and heartfelt, but somehow something else came out.

"Does the warden of the asylum know three of his patients are missing?"

Sofia giggled. "It's good to see the prospect of certain death hasn't wiped out your sense of humor."

"Well, you know my motto: If God hadn't intended for us to laugh all the time, he wouldn't have given Harvey that hair."

"I'm having second thoughts about having second thoughts," said Aidan.

"I'm glad you did," Jake replied.

"You said you had a plan, dude, what is it?"

Harvey and Sofia gathered beside Aidan in the center of the floor, waiting to hear Jake's great idea.

"What are they doing here, Jake? I thought we were doing this alone."

All three of them turned around. Eddie Tierney stood just behind them, under the upraised garage door.

"Get The Beast, Harvey," Aidan ordered. "Eddie here is going home with a couple of lumps on his head."

"No, hold up!" Jake shouted. Harvey took his hands away from the bat on the wall. "Eddie is helping us."

"Dude, we can't trust *him*," said Harvey in disbelief.

"*I* trust him," replied Jake. "Eddie knows everything."

Eddie pulled the door down behind him; it slammed shut with a loud metal screech.

"I know all about the Big Baresi," said Eddie, taking off his jacket and throwing it onto the couch. "I'm here to help."

"Jake, are you just going to let it go at that?" asked Aidan, more than a little astonished. "After what he did?"

"It's not important right now," Jake replied firmly. "When this is over, Eddie and me will figure things out, between *us*. So get used to it. We need Eddie."

Aidan shook his head and walked to the wall of the garage, the light from Jake's bare lamp threw his shadow onto the roof.

"Did you get them?" Jake asked Eddie.

"Yes, I've got them hidden away; just tell me where you need them."

"Did anyone see you?"

"No."

"Jake, what is going on?" Sofia couldn't take it any longer. "What's the plan, what has he hidden away, and what other surprises have you got lined up?"

Suddenly the garage door was yanked up again. Wedged in the opening, holding the door above their heads, were Demi and Desiree Dubble.

"All right, Drake, we believe you!" shouted Demi.

"No. Way." Aidan stared in astonishment. "You've got the Dubble Ds as well?"

The door dropped down with a metal clang as both sisters waddled into the room. Harvey stepped back against the wall beside Aidan as the twins squeezed past.

"Dude, I'd never noticed how small this garage was before."

Jake calmly remained seated as the Dubbles stopped right in front of his desk, infuriated and out of breath.

"We've just come from the prison," fumed Desiree, "and our mum said she's suspected all along that Cortesi was the one that grassed them up!"

"She said she didn't tell us," Demi continued, "because she was scared we might do something silly."

"As if you would." Jake smiled.

"I don't know what you're up to, Jake, but if it involves kicking Cortesi in the goolies, we're in!" Desiree nodded to her sister in agreement.

"Dude, please tell me they're not part of the plan," pleaded Harvey.

"Shut it, Shortcake," barked Demi, "or I'll kick yours so hard you'll be flashing them every time you smile."

"Okeydokey," Harvey squeaked, and turned to face the wall like a naughty school boy.

"I can't guarantee that you'll get to kick him," said Jake, grinning, "but if my plan works out like it should, you'll never have to see Cortesi ever again."

The Dubbles took some time to let the thought sink in.

"What would we have to do?" asked Demi suspiciously.

"All you have to do, ladies," replied Jake, "is be your normal, sexy selves."

Both sisters giggled coyly, while everyone else in the garage looked on in wonder.

"And help me get some information."

"All right, then," Desiree said as she and her sister walked to the couch, "we're all ears, tell us what this plan is."

Eddie stared wide-eyed at the twins as they stood over him, like a tiny rabbit caught between two humongous headlights.

"Budge up," said Demi, but before Eddie could move, both sisters sat down, trapping him between them in a flabby vise.

"Excellent." Jake looked at Eddie and smiled. "Now that we're all nice and comfy, I'll tell you my plan. It's bold, it's dangerous, but if we get away with it—"

"*If* we get away with it?" interrupted Sofia.

"If we get away with it, then the guys we're going after won't know what hit them!"

CHAPTER 21

There was no escaping the unease that hung in the air around Lochrannoch.

Ever since the name Baresi was first uttered in hushed conversations, the housing projects' residents knew that it would all end in bloodshed.

It always did.

The only certainty they had was that the battle was looming.

The wind whistled through the near-silent complex, whipping up dust clouds and rehousing litter to anywhere it cared to carry it.

Dark clouds gathered ominously in the skies above, as though everyone and everything were pulling up a chair and taking their seats for the main event.

The streets were almost deserted. Only the footsteps of the nervous could be heard as they hurried from where they were to where they were going.

Except for Fingers McGraw.

He hummed a tune loudly as he nonchalantly strolled through the streets, his hands in his jeans pockets.

His face looked weatherbeaten — the result of standing around on street corners since the age of seven, selling whatever he'd managed to knock off that day.

While other criminals belonged to gangs or crews, Fingers preferred to work alone.

He calmly checked his watch and smiled. The time was unimportant, it was the watch he had just pickpocketed from a businessman on the subway that filled his heart with bliss.

"Target acquired, dude." Harvey's voice crackled through Jake's hands-free earpiece.

"Thanks, Harvey, where is he?"

Harvey perched on the roof of a tenement building that looked down across the projects' courtyard.

In one hand he held a pair of large binoculars that were so heavy he could only hold them to his eyes for a matter of seconds; in the other was his mobile phone.

"He's coming from the underpass, heading past the apartments toward the shops."

Jake immediately started the engine and crunched it into gear. A large section of the trailer's crushed metal roof flipped skyward as the truck lurched forward, before clanging back down again.

"I'm bringing it around," said Jake. A thin white wire to his mobile phone, nestled in his inside pocket, was connected to his earpiece.

Harvey lifted his binoculars to his eyes and struggled to find the magnified face of Fingers. Suddenly the ratlike features of McGraw filled his vision at 800 X magnification.

"Wow! That's not good," Harvey shouted as he dropped the binoculars and picked up his phone.

Jake hit the brakes.

"What is it?" he panicked.

"Mega dandruff problem," replied Harvey. "It's like snowflakes on his collar."

Jake let out a breath and shook his head. The stick shift crunched and he was on the move again.

"I've lost him, dude, he's taken the road behind the projects. *Adios, amigo.*"

Jake heard Harvey hang up in his ear; instantly his phone started ringing again.

"Do you see him, Aidan?" he asked as he answered.

"Yeah, I've got him," Aidan replied, watching from the shadows of an apartment doorway.

"He's coming straight toward me."

Jake forced the stick shift into second and prodded harder on the accelerator. The engine's hum dipped momentarily before the truck picked up the pace.

"Hang on, Jake, he's crossing the road toward the canal path!"

Jake lifted his foot off the pedal and listened for Aidan's commentary.

"He's vaulted the fence . . . walking down the embankment . . . he isn't going to the shops; he must be heading for the main road."

Jake slammed on the brakes and spun the steering wheel in his hands. The truck swung around in a wide circle, its fat tires thumping up onto the sidewalk, then screeching back down onto the road.

"He'll get off the path near the railroad tracks, Jake; you have to get there before him."

"I'm on it," Jake replied, stomping on the accelerator.

"I've lost sight of him, Jake. Good luck."

Aidan clicked off. Jake rubbed his hands against his jacket to dry some sweat. His phone started ringing yet again.

"Jake, it's me," said Eddie. "Fingers is still on the embankment."

"How close is he to the tracks?" Jake asked.

Eddie looked out from under a large umbrella on the opposite side of the canal. A fishing rod lay at his feet.

"About a hundred feet. Where are you?"

"Not close enough," Jake replied, crunching into a higher gear, demanding more speed.

"Jake, you'll have to get that truck parked before he reaches the top of the stairs at the end of the path!"

Jake weaved the truck through some parked cars and turned down a street that ran parallel with the canal.

"I see you," Eddie informed him as he watched Jake speed down the road.

"Where is Fingers?" shouted Jake.

"Sixty feet from the stairs."

"Count them down," Jake urged him, pressing as hard as he could on the accelerator. He could see the top of the stairs up ahead on his left. The stairs that Fingers would soon be climbing.

"Fifty feet," Eddie notified him.

The road Jake was on turned sharply to the right, directly across from the stairs.

"Slow down, man, or you'll go right off the road—you'll never make that turn."

Jake ignored him. "How far now?"

"Thirty feet."

Jake grabbed the wheel tightly in both hands. The truck thundered toward the turn as down below on the canal Fingers neared the bottom of the stairs.

A SLOW sign zoomed past the windshield as Jake reached the turn and yanked the steering wheel around with both hands. The tires squealed in protest as the cab veered across the road, the trailer swaying violently behind it, threatening to topple over, as Jake held on with all his might.

"He's climbing the stairs now!"

The groan of strained metal screamed out as the tires grappled for grip on the concrete.

"Halfway up the stairs."

The steering wheel zipped through Jake's hands as the truck straightened up, and he slammed on the brakes, juddering to a stop beside the curb. Quickly he pulled on the emergency brake and shut off the engine.

"He's at the top, Jake, I've lost him. Get out now." Eddie hung up.

The truck shuddered into silence as Fingers's head appeared at the top of the stairs.

Jake looked up and saw Fingers behind him in the sideview mirror. Quickly he dived onto the passenger seat, out of sight.

His phone started ringing.

"Jake, he's right behind you," panicked Sofia as he answered. She had a lofty view of the rear driver's side of the truck, from a stairwell window.

Fingers stood in the middle of the deserted road, staring suspiciously at the truck.

"Hello, darling," he muttered under his breath. "We meet again."

Tentatively he moved toward the rear door of the trailer, his eyes darting around warily with every step.

"He's moving toward the back door," Sofia squeaked, the tension and dread stretching her vocal cords to the snapping point.

Stuck in the cab, Jake lay across the driver and passenger seats, his heart pounding heavily as he tried to figure out a method of escape.

Fingers could hear the trailer creaking as the metal settled. Slowly he lifted the locking handle: It gave a sharp screech, almost jolting Jake onto the floor.

Fingers took one last look behind him before he pulled the door open. An over-inflated sumo suit tumbled on top of him as more wedged in the trailer door and threatened to escape.

"Jake, how are you going to get out?" Sofia whispered into her phone, as though Fingers might hear her.

"I don't know," Jake replied, the distress clear in his voice.

"He's coming toward you, Jake!"

"Which side?"

"The driver's side!"

Fingers cautiously walked beside the trailer toward the front of the truck.

Jake crouched in front of the passenger seat, below the window.

Fingers walked straight past the driver's door to the front, and looked up at the cracked windshield.

"He's at the front of the truck, Jake!"

A piece of the front grille twisted outward, severed from its normal housing: a visual reminder of Jake's recent police chase.

"He's going back toward the driver's door."

Fingers stopped by the door. Looking around, he raised his arm over his shoulder and tried the handle.

Jake looked on in horror as the door popped open a little.

Fingers felt the door give as he scrutinized the area around the truck. Smiling, he turned and jumped into the cab.

The front was empty.

He looked behind the seats into the rear of the cab.

Nothing there, either.

Wasting no time, he felt for the keys. They were still in the ignition.

"My lucky day!" He laughed as the engine burst into life.

"Jake, can you hear me? Are you OK? Can you answer?" urged Sofia, looking down at the truck from the stairwell.

Jake didn't reply.

Black clouds of diesel smoke burst from the exhaust as Fingers revved the engine.

"Jake, answer me! Jump out of the cab and run, just run!"

The brake lights flashed on as the wheels slowly turned, and Fingers pulled away.

"Jake!" Sofia screamed, her voice echoing down the empty stairs.

As the trailer pulled away, Jake appeared underneath it, lying flat on his back in the road.

"Oh God, no! What happened?" yelled Sofia. "Jake!"

The truck sped away, and within seconds turned the corner at the end of the street and was gone.

Jake opened his eyes, looked up at the stairwell window, and smiled.

"What happened?" Jake replied, laughing. "Fingers took the bait, that's what happened."

"I'm going to kill you, Drake!"

"Yeah, well, get in line," he replied as he picked himself up and dusted the dirt from his jacket. "So far, so good, it's all going according to plan. Now call the Dubbles and tell them to text Fingers from an unknown number. They need to send the message now!"

CHAPTER 22

Fingers McGraw rested his head against the steering wheel and wondered how he'd managed to get mixed up with Baresi.

The gentle thrum of the engine pulsed through the wheel; it would have proved soothing if Fingers hadn't been beyond calming at that point in time.

He'd only made it a little more than two miles away when the phone in his pocket started to beep. Up until then he couldn't believe his luck at getting back the stolen truck with its load still in the trailer, even if it was minus the money.

He'd laughed, punched the roof of the cab, turned the stereo up loud, and even contemplated calling Cortesi and telling him the sumo suit deal was back on.

Now he sat in the truck in silence, on a stretch of empty road facing a dead end.

His phone lit up as he opened the text message:

> I have given u ur truck back. I want 2 work with u.
> I will buy the suits from u as a sign of good will.
> DO NOT SELL THEM 2 ANY1 ELSE. Do not touch the cargo.
> It was easy 2 find u. Do not disappoint me.
> I will b in touch soon with instructions. — Baresi

Fingers threw his phone onto the dashboard and sighed.

CHAPTER 23

John Joseph Scullen heard the morning paper drop through his door's mail slot.

He raised his head from under the covers and looked at his alarm clock. It was only ten minutes to six in the morning.

"He's early," he mumbled as he turned and snuggled into his pillow, closing his eyes.

It was only a matter of seconds before his suspicious mind forced them open again, and he turned back to the clock.

Slowly he sat up and pulled off the covers. He was wearing his usual bedtime attire: a pair of jeans and a T-shirt—not great for sleeping, but just right for a fast getaway. His feet found his sneakers and his hand found a hammer nestled under his pillow. Armed and ready, he pulled back the bedroom door and edged out into the hallway.

Just behind his front door lay a copy of that morning's newspaper.

"You're too suspicious, J.J." He smiled as he walked over and picked up the paper. A white envelope with a red letter *B* fell from inside it and landed next to his feet.

Scullen raised an eyebrow as he looked down at it, then picked it up and tore it open.

Enclosed was a typed letter addressed to him.

Dear Mr. Scullen,

We have never met before, but I hope that situation may change soon.

I am aware of your reason for returning to Lochrannoch, and I can help you acquire what you're looking for.

You may be suspicious of me, as I am of you, but an example of my good intentions awaits you tomorrow at Cowell's Fruit Market, West Clyde Street.

Please arrive promptly at 11 a.m.

I look forward to working with you to resolve our mutual problem.

Yours sincerely,

Baresi

Scullen rubbed his hand over his face and stared out the window. A small redheaded boy passed by, carrying a luminous orange bag over his shoulder.

Scullen watched as his mail slot opened and another copy of that morning's newspaper landed on his carpet.

The light smattering of rain did little to dampen the enthusiasm of the kids playing soccer outside Bruno Aziz's Mini-Mart.

A makeshift goal had been drawn in paint on the long line of steel protective window shutters that kept bricks and bottles at bay, encouraging continual bangs and clangs as the ball bounced off it, and the game was played out.

A silver Ford Mondeo pulled up beside them.

Instantly the kids started whistling and jeering as the car rolled to a stop.

It was easy to spot an unmarked police car. No wheel trims, subtle paint, four doors, and two arrogant-looking plonkers in the front seats.

"Beat it!" snarled Chief Stone as he hauled his overweight posterior from the passenger seat.

The kids scarpered, some on skateboards and some on foot.

Jake was far enough away not to be spotted but close enough to hear the words "muppets," "tools," and "jackholes" among the barrage of jeering as the kids continued their heckling of the local arm of the law.

Jake lifted his mountain bike from the grass mound at the top of the hill and climbed on.

Officer Surpress joined his colleague Stone at the front of the car, muttering and cursing the kids, before they marched into the Mini-Mart and out of sight.

Jake's back wheel spun on the grass as he powered over the mound and down the other side of the hill, pedaling as fast as he could.

The wind slapped his face as he shot down the hill toward the shop at the bottom.

By now he was traveling so fast he didn't need to pedal; the wheels were turning quicker than the pedals could make them go.

Dirt from the wet grass flicked into the air behind him as he prepared to pull on the brakes. The bike's tires bounced up onto the sidewalk, and Jake squeezed the brakes as hard as he could. The rear tire spun around violently; gravel sprayed the side of the police car as the skid came to a stop.

Jake hurriedly reached into his jacket and pulled a white envelope from the pocket. He lifted up a windshield-wiper blade and tucked the envelope behind it before taking off once again on his bike. Reaching the end of the sidewalk, he veered behind the shops.

Chief Stone threw open the shop door and hurried out onto the sidewalk, looking around.

"What's going on?" asked Officer Surpress, following his boss outside.

"I don't know," answered Stone, "but someone is up to something."

"It was probably just a bored kid making a crank call. It's not the first time we've been called out to a break-in only to find there hasn't been one."

Chief Stone wasn't convinced. He paced the sidewalk, looking around.

"Hang on!" The police chief stopped beside the car and stared at the envelope. Slowly his eyes scanned the grassy hills around the shops. He lifted the envelope and turned it over.

It had a red letter *B* on it.

"Get in the car now!"

Officer Surpress rushed to the driver's door and climbed into the car beside Stone.

"What is it?" he asked urgently.

"It's a letter from Baresi. I knew I smelt a rat."

"Open it."

Stone tore the envelope open and pulled a typed letter from inside.

"'Dear Chief Stone and Officer Surpress,'" he read. "'You will no doubt be aware that the balance of power is changing in Lochrannoch. If you are smart, you will change with it.'"

"What does he mean by that?" asked Surpress.

"He's looking to get us on his side," Stone replied before turning back to the letter.

"'I understand that you have a special understanding with others in my line of business. I would like to propose a new relationship that will undoubtedly prove more fruitful for us both. As a token of my goodwill, I have arranged a gift for you both.'"

"A gift?" interrupted Surpress. "What gift?"

Stone finished reading the letter, then folded it and placed it in his pocket.

"It doesn't say," he replied, "but he's given us an address and a time to pick it up tomorrow."

Surpress looked confused. He started the car and pulled on his seat belt.

"Do you think we can trust him?" he asked.

"I don't know," answered Stone, "but if he does get control of everything, we'd be stupid not to get in with him. Besides, I like getting presents, don't you?"

Surpress placed the gearshift into first and checked his mirror.

"I don't know," he replied. "I've got a bad feeling about this."

"Come on!" Stone laughed. "What's the worst that could happen? We're a couple of coppers. We're untouchable."

CHAPTER 24

Beep-beep. *Beep-beep. Beep-beep.*

The alarm clock had been sounding for almost fifteen seconds before Jake mustered the energy to raise his arm from beneath the covers and slap it across the room.

He hadn't had a good night's sleep. Like a soldier about to go into battle, he'd lain awake worrying and fretting about what might happen the next day.

He had made the arrangements he needed to make, all except one, and briefed his friends countless times on the dangers they would face. He knew exactly what he had to do and when, but he couldn't shake the thought that very few things ever go entirely according to plan.

Jake groaned as he rolled over. The sunlight streamed through his flimsy curtains and shone directly into his eyes.

He blinked some sleep away and looked at the time on his clock; it read eight-thirty.

His clothes were neatly folded on his chair under the window; the clothes-selection exercise had been undertaken in the early hours of the morning in a desperate bid to tire himself out. It hadn't worked.

It had been shortly after five o'clock when tiredness eventually took control and sent Jake off to the land of nod.

Now he was being dragged back to reality. Abruptly.

Jake allowed himself the luxury of a few minutes' calm to wake up properly. His back cracked at the first stretch and yawn of the day.

Jake looked up at the ceiling. The nerves and mild panic he'd felt last night hadn't awakened inside him yet, so he enjoyed a moment without fear.

He felt alive. He felt contented. He felt a strange hand on his ankle.

He felt a strange hand on his ankle!

"What the . . ." Jake jerked his leg away and sat up suddenly, hitting the wall.

"Do not worry, Master Drake," the soft voice whispered quietly in a broken accent, "and do not scream; we do not want to wake your dear grandmother, do we?"

The man at the bottom of Jake's bed smiled at him.

His long black hair stopped just short of his shoulders, and his eyes were the most amazing shade of green that Jake had ever seen.

An immaculately tailored suit hung from his tall, muscular frame.

"Who are you? What do you want?" Jake asked in terror.

"You know who I am," the man replied, his piercing eyes staring back at Jake. "My name is Baresi."

"That's impossible," said Jake, shaking his head. "You can't be!"

"What . . . you think because you made me up that I did not already exist?"

Jake recoiled and tried to take in what was happening.

"You are not a good boy, Jake Drake, but you are not a bad boy, either. I know in your heart you have *good intentions*."

"What do you want from me?" asked Jake.

The man stood up and walked toward the window.

"You have a very big day ahead of you, Jake, a very big day indeed. A lot of people want to kill you and me. Now if it was my choice, I would kill all of those people in an instant. . . ."

The sharp click of his fingers resonated through Jake; he wasn't expecting it.

"But it is not up to me. Today you have control, Jake. You must do what you know is right, but if your work does not go as planned, you have to kill them all or they will kill you."

"I can't kill them!" exclaimed Jake.

The man turned and quickly paced the floor toward him; Jake pulled his legs up toward his chest; Baresi's hand grabbed for Jake's throat —

Beep-beep. Beep-beep. Beep-beep.

Jake awoke suddenly and looked at his alarm clock. The time was eight-thirty.

He took a deep breath and stopped the alarm.

His head nestled back into his pillow, which was damp with sweat.

"It was just a dream." He sighed with relief. "What a time to start cracking up!"

Jake looked across his bedroom; it was exactly as it had been in his dream. The sun penetrated the curtains with a bright diffused light, his chair sat beneath the window with his clothes neatly piled on it, and he could feel a hand on his ankle.

Help! he thought. *Who's that?*

Pharrp.

"Oh, it's just you, Gran," said Jake, sitting up. "I didn't hear you come in."

"Good morning, Jake," said his grandmother. "I thought I'd better come and wake you before you slept the whole day away."

"It's Saturday, Gran, and it's only half past eight," Jake replied.

"Only!" His gran laughed. "When I was your age, I used to wake up at five in the morning, jump out of bed, take a deep breath, and . . ."

Pharrp.

". . . breathe in a new day."

Jake ignored the obvious joke.

"Will you be able to get me a few groceries from the shop today, Jake? I'd go myself but it's a dangerous neighborhood for an old lady."

"Of course I will," he replied. "I've just got some things to do first, and then I'll get you what you need."

"You're good to your old granny," she said, rubbing Jake's cheek. "You're not an angel, mind, and you're not a devil, either, but you've got a good heart with *good intentions.*"

Jake took his grandmother's hand and held it tight.

"So I've heard," he mumbled.

"What?"

"Nothing, Grandma."

Jake's grandmother slowly raised herself from Jake's bed and shuffled to the door.

"You know what, Gran?" Jake suddenly shouted after her. His grandmother turned around to face him. "I've never really said it before, but I've always wanted to."

"Say what, Jake?"

Jake felt a lump in his throat.

"Say thanks. I've never really said thanks for everything you've done for me. I want to say it now, Gran. I want you to know how grateful I am, and how all I've ever wanted to do was the right thing. I know it didn't always turn out that way."

A look of fear crept across Jake's grandmother's face.

"It sounds like you're saying good-bye, Jake."

"Of course I'm not," he replied. "Where would I be going, eh? No, I just wanted to tell you how much you mean to me."

A single tear slid down his grandmother's cheek.

"Oh, Jake," she said, beaming, "that's lovely!"

Pharrp.

"Just lovely!"

The bedroom door swished closed and Jake heard his grandmother whimper and fart her way back up the hall.

"All right, then," he said aloud, "let's do this."

Jake picked up his mobile and scrolled through his personal numbers until the name Eddie appeared on his screen.

It hardly rang before it was answered.

"Did you get it?" Jake asked, climbing from the bed and walking to his window.

"What," Eddie replied, "the van?"

"No, the joke I told last night. . . . Yes, of course, the van!" Jake pulled open the curtains, shaking his head in exasperation.

"Well, there was a slight hitch."

Jake stopped still.

"What hitch? Have you got the van or not?"

"Yes and no," replied Eddie cagily. "I've got *a* van."

"Don't tell me," said Jake resolutely. "I don't want to know. Just don't be late."

CHAPTER 25

"**W**ill you lot just huwwy up!"

Franco Cortesi's voice boomed over the noise inside the garage as all around him men picked up their guns and collected ammunition from a crate in the center of the floor.

Cortesi stood back from the mayhem in a corner of the garage. His not inconsiderable mass was cloaked in a knee-length brown suede overcoat; in his right hand he carried a brown suitcase.

"I told you two to get pwofessionals," he sneered at Tweedle-Dumb and Tweedle-Dumber.

"Boss, why don't I carry the briefcase for you?" Tweedle-Dumb rubbed his mustache as he eyed the case.

Cortesi glared at him from the corner of his eye.

"The case is pewfectly OK; now get these men into the cars!"

Dumb and Dumber hurried across the service bay, shouting instructions to the men.

In the center of the floor, in puddles of oil and water, were the remains of the 1958 Mercury Turnpike Cruiser, which for years had hung from the rafters. Its twin headlights lay in pieces and its chrome grille had been bent open on purpose.

Tweedle-Dumb looked down at the mess in front of him.

"All this time," he muttered to his colleague, "the jewels were right above our heads."

The men finished loading their guns with ammunition. Bullets slid into chambers as they cocked them and flicked on the safety catches.

In the distance, the faint chime of an ice cream van could be heard.

The sound got louder.

Cortesi stopped barking orders and listened as the chimes increased in volume and the van got closer.

Tweedle-Dumb and Dumber stopped picking their ammunition from the crate and listened as the rumble of a speeding van joined the tune.

"What the heck is that?" muttered Dumber.

The chimes got louder as the van hurtled down the hill toward Cortesi's. The noise inside the garage died away, replaced by a tense silence that somehow seemed just as loud.

Suddenly a blue-and-white ice cream van swung into the service bay and skidded to a stop in front of Cortesi. Its chime echoed off the bare brick walls.

Instantly the men took up position: Some jumped from vehicles and others took cover behind steel racking. All of them trained their guns on the van.

Cortesi stepped back and strained to see who was in the driver's seat. Through the dirty windshield he saw a man in a black coat and wide-brimmed hat. The collar was pulled up around his face and the hat pulled down, obscuring his eyes.

With a warped gurgle the chime stopped, and a loud burst of microphone feedback belched around the garage as the speaker was flicked on.

"Please don't shoot me!" came a distorted voice. There was another man in the passenger seat quavering into the microphone. "They'll blow us all up if you shoot. They have my wife and kids. They said they would kill them if I didn't drive this van into the garage and demand the diamonds. This van is full of C4 plastic explosive."

The side window opened and a large green duffel bag was thrown from the shadows behind the counter. It landed on the concrete floor with a muffled thud.

A few men cried out and dived for cover, half-expecting the bag to explode.

"The bag is full of explosives. If I don't drive out of here in forty seconds' time with the diamonds, they'll blow up this van. If I drive out of here with an empty case, they'll blow up the bag."

The driver's window creaked as he quickly rolled it down. In his outstretched hand he clutched a brown package. On top of it was a small digital display with a red and green light, and two thin red wires ran underneath the paper casing.

"This is three pounds of C4; it's enough to blow up this whole garage."

Cortesi reeled farther away from the van.

"This van has thirty pounds of explosives. It will blow up in exactly . . . twenty-two seconds unless you give me the diamonds. Please, Mr. Cortesi, just give me the diamonds or we will all die!"

Cortesi looked around the garage at the men. Fear was etched on every face staring back at him, urging him to hand over the stones.

"Fifteen seconds. Mr. Cortesi, *please* throw the case through the side window."

Cortesi quickly walked to the side of the van and hurled the case through the open window. It bounced off a box of sour-cream-and-onion potato chips and landed in the ice cream freezer.

"Tell these wotters that I will twack them down and muwder evewy one of them!"

Cortesi's voice reached an all-new glass-shattering level of anger.

A crunching of gears ripped through the air as the van edged its way out into the daylight.

Cortesi watched as it slowly reversed; then in a cloud of blue smoke and a burst of *plink plonk* chimes it screeched back up the hill away from him.

"Don't just stand there!" he squealed. "Go after that ice cweam van!"

The noise in the garage switched from stunned silence to organized chaos as the men rushed to the nearest car. Guns were checked and double-checked for ammunition as a symphony of revving engines and slamming doors escaped from the vast bays into the street outside.

Franco Cortesi was the last man in. He slammed the rear door of his Jaguar and pulled a silver handgun from inside his long coat.

"What are you waiting for?" yelled Cortesi at the long willowy neck of Tweedle-Dumb in the driver's seat.

"I think you should take a look behind you, Boss," his minion replied, glancing in his rearview mirror.

The car shook from side to side as Cortesi maneuvered his bulky body around to see behind him. Three submachine gun barrels were pointing through the window straight at his head. Cortesi flicked off the safety catch on his own gun and cocked the trigger back.

"Don't do it, Boss," Tweedle-Dumb said quietly. "They're everywhere. They'll shoot us dead in the cars before we even get a round off."

Cortesi looked out his side window. Surrounding every vehicle were masked men with semiautomatic weapons. Their guns were trained on the faces of Cortesi's men, their fingers on the triggers.

"It's Mickey Chang," said Tweedle-Dumb, making an extra special effort to remain perfectly still. "His limousine has just pulled in."

Cortesi slipped his gun inside his pocket and opened the door.

Behind his own car sat the long black vintage Mercedes of Mickey Chang, its engine humming quietly.

Cortesi walked toward the open window at the back, but stopped a few feet away. His finger nervously rubbed the trigger of the gun inside his pocket.

"I'm vewy disappointed, Mister Chang!" he shouted into the darkness of the car. "What happened to our awwangement?"

"Don't be too disappointed," the soft voice of Mickey Chang answered. "Things could be worse—you could be dead already!"

Cortesi's nostrils flared open as if he was trying to breathe in as much cool air as possible to quell his burning rage.

"Just give me the diamonds," said Chang quietly.

"You're too late," Cortesi fumed. "They have alweady been stolen—just two minutes ago—and wight now you're stopping me fwom getting them back."

"Stop talking nonsense," Chang replied. "Just give me the rocks or . . . Hold on. . . . What's that? Cortesi, you'll have to wait a minute, my brother is speaking to me."

Cortesi stood anxiously staring into the darkness of the limousine, listening to Mickey Chang arguing with his dead brother.

"My brother, Jimmy, says I should shoot you in the face, but I explained that if you're dead you can't tell me where the diamonds are. It's much better if I torture you mercilessly."

"I have alweady told you, they're gone!"

"So who has the gems then?" Mickey Chang demanded from the darkness of his car.

"Look, Boss!" Tweedle-Dumb hurried toward the limousine carrying the green duffel bag that had been thrown from the van.

"Are you mental?" Cortesi screamed. "That's full of explosives!"

The bag thumped onto the hood of the Mercedes. Tweedle-Dumb flipped it over and emptied the contents on top of the car. Hundreds of Baresi calling cards spilled across the metal and down to the floor.

"I knew it!" shouted Cortesi. "It was Bawesi inside that ice cweam van!"

Cortesi ran back toward his own car and yanked open the door.

"Back up!" he screamed at Chang's limousine.

"Boss, how will we know which way the van went?" asked Tweedle-Dumb, climbing into the front seat.

"We'll follow the tune. Just listen out for 'Wudolph the Wed-Nosed Weindeer.'"

CHAPTER 26

"**H**arvey, for the last time, I do not want a cone, with or without sprinkles on top!"

Jake shook his head as the ice cream van hurtled down the road, its chimes blaring at full volume. His wide-brimmed hat dropped down over his eyes, forcing him to swerve into the oncoming lane before he nudged it back up and steadied his course.

"Dude, I was only asking," Harvey replied with his head deep inside the freezer, a little muffled and miffed.

Aidan and Sofia stumbled around in the back of the van as Jake weaved through the streets.

"Any luck with the briefcase, Eddie?" Jake shouted over his shoulder as he crunched another gear.

"I'm still working on it," Eddie replied, sitting on the floor with the case between his legs. His fingers worked nimbly as he tried to pry open the locks.

"I can't believe this was the only van you could get; it handles terribly."

The gears crunched again as Jake tried to coax some more speed.

"Yeah, it does," mumbled Eddie, his attention still focused on the case, "especially when you drive like a girl."

"Shut it, Eddie!" snapped Sofia, picking chocolate cookie crumbs from her hair.

"What's the time?" Jake asked.

Aidan looked at his watch. "Five minutes to eleven."

"Good. We're right on schedule."

"Dude, we have a problem," said Harvey, climbing down from the freezer with ice cream in his eyebrows.

"What is it now?" Jake wiped some sweat from his forehead.

Harvey placed his hand on Jake's shoulder.

"We're all out of vanilla, and the mint chocolate chip is seriously low."

CHAPTER 27

The noise of the truck reverberated down the empty side street as Fingers McGraw inched down the road at a snail's pace.

He looked around the street suspiciously and continually checked his mirrors for any sign that the Big Baresi was watching him.

A lone stray dog darted along the deserted pavement in front of the appointed warehouse. Fingers stopped the tractor trailer and a gust from the air brakes escaped loudly before the whole truck shook itself still as he turned off the engine.

His breathing was heavy and his heart was racing as he lifted his mobile phone and scrolled his text.

Cowell's Fruit Market, West Clyde St, Glasgow. B there at 11:10 a.m. Park across rear entrance bay. Enter via red metal door. Come alone. — Baresi

Fingers opened the truck door and slid down from the seat to the pavement below.

The faint murmur of distant traffic reminded him that he was a long way from being able to be heard, should he scream for help.

The street was eerily silent as he walked toward the red metal door. Nervously he glanced over his shoulder. The whole place was deserted.

The lock on the door had been forced open. Shavings of metal lay around his feet as Fingers cautiously pulled the door open and peered inside.

Sections of the vast concrete floor were reflected in puddles as the daylight streamed through the huge glass windows near the top of the warehouse's high walls.

Fingers took one step inside. The door closed quietly behind him, leaving him in the shadows.

"Hello," his halfhearted shout echoed across the warehouse, "is there anyone here?"

Jake skidded the van to a sudden stop beside the phone booth.

Boxes of candy and chocolate bars flew through the air, showering Aidan, Sofia, and Eddie in a confectionary downpour.

Harvey, too, would have been caught in the deluge had he not returned to his favorite position: head down, butt sticking up out of the freezer.

"Harvey, it's time to make the call," said Jake.

Harvey wriggled out backward, his face barely recognizable underneath a layer of strawberry, mint chocolate chip, and vanilla ice cream, and slid down the confectionary mountain to the floor.

"Dude," he replied wearily, "I don't feel so good."

"Well, you shouldn't have scoffed all the ice cream!" said Jake unsympathetically. "Now get yourself out there and make the call."

"Why don't I just use this phone?" asked Harvey, picking up Sofia's mobile from the dashboard.

"Because it has to be a pay phone; the police can trace a call from a cell," replied Jake as he snatched the phone and tossed it into the glove compartment. "Now get going."

"I think I'm going to be sick," balked Harvey.

"Move!" The choral command rang out as all of his friends dragged him to his feet and shoved him out the door.

"Remember, muffle the mouthpiece and ask for Officer Telford"—Jake clung to the open door — "then get over to the warehouse as quick as you can and help the others."

Jake closed the door and jumped back into the driver's seat.

"What's the time now?" he asked, pulling away from the curb.

"Just gone ten past eleven," Sofia answered.

"I don't believe it," Eddie said in astonishment. "Check this out."

"Oh my God," Sofia muttered.

Jake looked over his shoulder into the back of the van.

Eddie kneeled in the center of the floor; the brown leather briefcase was pried open at his knees. Aidan and Sofia crouched over him. Small reflections of light twinkled across their astounded expressions as Eddie slowly turned the case around toward Jake.

In the soft leather-trimmed lining were three million dollars' worth of glistening, brilliantly cut diamonds.

"Jake — the road!" yelled Aidan.

The van swerved from side to side as Jake over-steered away from the oncoming traffic toward the cars parked at the side of the street, before finally correcting the steering and regaining control.

"We're nearly there," he said, trying to get another glimpse of the stones in his rearview mirror. "Get ready, guys."

Aidan and Sofia slowly stood up and walked to the front of the van, their eyes fixed on the diamonds like two hypnotized zombies.

"There's the truck," said Jake, slowing the van to a stop.

Out the side window they saw the stolen truck in front of Cowell's Fruit Market, where Fingers had parked it.

Jake slowly turned down the street as Eddie closed the briefcase and joined the others at the front.

"You know what to do," said Jake. The van rolled up behind the rig and stopped. "As many as you can. Just squash them in."

Sofia quietly opened the door and stepped down into the street, followed by Eddie.

"Remember, keep going until we tell you to stop." Jake smiled nervously at Sofia.

"We will," she said, smiling back. "Be careful."

Aidan pulled the door closed on them.

"Let's finish this."

"What are you doing, Aidan? Get out!" said Jake.

"We're doing this together," Aidan replied. "I'm not letting you go in there alone."

"Aidan, you don't have to do this. You can't."

Aidan opened his jacket to let Jake see what he was wearing. "Yes, I can, I've got protection. Now let's get this van around to the front."

"All right, then, let's do it!" Jake laughed.

Fingers spun around nervously in the direction of the sound.

"Who's there?" he asked anxiously.

A rat scurried out of the shadows and across the floor away from him.

Fingers breathed again.

All the way along the extensive sidewall were separate gaps leading into adjoining warehouses that made up the once-bustling fruit market.

Fingers edged farther inside the rear warehouse and listened tensely.

"Is this some kind of a joke?"

The unexpected voice threw Fingers as he stumbled toward it, into the shadows.

Out of the darkness stepped the hulking figure of John Joseph Scullen.

"I know you're not him. Who are you working with?" he asked angrily, pacing the warehouse toward Fingers.

"Nobody, I've done exactly as you asked, Mr. Baresi."

Scullen stopped dead in his tracks.

"What did you call me?"

Fingers stepped back uncertainly.

"I'm sorry; don't you want me to call you Baresi, Mr. Baresi?"

Scullen looked around the shadows of the abandoned warehouse.

"Who told you to come here?" he snapped angrily at Fingers.

"You did."

"I am not Baresi!" Scullen yelled. His voice echoed off the bare walls.

"I-I don't understand," Fingers stuttered nervously. "I was told to come here and meet Baresi. I thought you were him."

"I was told the same thing," Scullen spoke under his breath as his eyes scoured the warehouse. "I think we've been set up."

The smashing of a door shattered the air in an adjoining warehouse, and the loud tinkling chimes of an ice cream van screamed around the vast empty space.

"What was that?" cried Fingers as he ran behind Scullen.

"I don't know," Scullen answered, "but it's coming from the front entrance."

"Are you all right?" Jake shouted to Aidan as the van skidded to a stop in the center of the floor. The loud jingling chimes bounced off the walls of the warehouse and they could hardly hear themselves think.

"Yeah, I'm fine," Aidan shouted back, the blood draining from his knuckles as both his hands clung on to the dashboard, "although I don't remember crashing through a door ever getting mentioned in the planning stage."

"I improvised," Jake replied, opening the passenger door and pushing Aidan out.

"What about the diamonds, Jake?" mouthed Aidan over the noise. He picked himself up from the dusty floor.

Jake jumped down beside him with the case in his hands. He placed it on the front seat and opened it. The diamonds sparkled darkly as the dim light from the warehouse refracted through them.

"We stick to the plan. We leave them," Jake replied solemnly. "They're the only things incriminating everyone. They need to be here when the cops arrive."

"It would have been good, though, if we could have kept them." Aidan grinned.

"Too right. But we have to go now, I saw the cops parked outside. They're instructed to come in here at exactly twenty minutes past. After our entrance they'll be dying to get in and see what's going on."

Jake and Aidan sprinted across the concrete floor toward a set of steel stairs rising up the huge sidewall.

"Can you see anything?" Fingers whispered in Scullen's ear as he peered around a doorway into the adjoining warehouse.

Scullen edgily stepped inside and looked around him.

"There's an ice cream van in the center of the floor," he quietly replied. "Looks like it's been abandoned."

A loud metal crash resonated above their heads.

"What was that?" asked Fingers.

Scullen looked up and saw the door at the top of the stairs bounce off the handrail and clang shut.

"Someone's just gone up onto the roof."

The chimes continued to echo down the expansive emptiness of the warehouse as Scullen walked cautiously toward the van.

Fingers McGraw looked on from the shadows as Scullen reached inside the driver's door. The chimes suddenly died.

"Well?" Fingers yelled. "What's going on?"

Scullen didn't reply. He stood staring into the van in stunned silence.

"Hey, big guy, what's going on?"

"I don't believe it," Scullen mumbled. "The diamonds."

"What did you say?" Fingers strained to hear.

"Baresi has given me the diamonds!"

"Diamonds?" Fingers yelled as he scurried from the shadows like a hungry rat. "What diamonds?"

Scullen lifted a handful of stones and let them fall through his fingers like sand.

"This is to show his *good intentions*," he said, mesmerized by the twinkling stones.

"Wow." Fingers appeared from behind him and stood gawping at the gems. "How will we split them?"

Scullen turned his head to Fingers.

"*We* won't split them. I did time for these diamonds; they're mine."

Suddenly a silver car plowed through the enormous hole in the doors; its tires squealed as it sped toward the van, skidding sideward in front of Scullen. A strip of flashing blue lights danced across the front of its grille.

"Back away from the van!" shouted Officer Surpress, climbing from the driver's seat, pointing a gun. "Don't do anything silly, Scullen."

Fingers McGraw backed away toward the front of the van.

"Or would you prefer us to call you Baresi?" asked Chief Stone as he ambled from his seat and walked around the car.

"So you pulled a number on Cortesi, eh? Nicked the diamonds from him?"

"I'm not Baresi," Scullen replied, holding his arms out away from his body. "You've got the wrong guy."

"Well, that minor detail hasn't stopped us before, has it, Officer Surpress?" scoffed Stone.

"You should know all about that, J.J."

Scullen sneered and turned his face away.

"It's true," whimpered Fingers, "he isn't Baresi; we've been set up."

"How many times has that happened to you?" replied Surpress. "Every time I arrest you, you've been set up."

"This time it's true!" shouted Fingers, but his pleas fell on deaf ears.

"So you're saying that you are not Baresi?" Stone interrogated Scullen.

"I told you I'm not."

Stone looked across to his corrupt colleague in confusion.

"So you can return the diamonds to your boss, Franco Cortesi," said Scullen scornfully.

"No, that's not the plan," sneered Surpress. "It seems Mr. Baresi has offered these diamonds to us as a gift, and you are the fall guy: a token arrest."

"But it's your lucky day, Scullen," Stone continued, "because today we officially retired ourselves from the police force, so we won't be arresting you, just killing you!" He leveled his gun at the big man's chest.

Scullen lowered his arms to his side, like a cornered animal accepting its fate.

"Now, Officer Surpress, pick up our pension."

Surpress shuffled toward the diamonds, but before he reached the briefcase a Jaguar zoomed into the warehouse followed by a cavalcade of cars.

"It's Cortesi!" shouted Surpress.

"And Mickey Chang," replied Stone as a black vintage Mercedes limousine slipped through the entrance and crossed the space between them.

The cars circled the ice cream van before branching off and stopping.

Scullen, Fingers, Stone, and Surpress watched as all around them men jumped from the cars holding semiautomatic weapons in their hands.

"This doesn't look good." Fingers whistled under his breath.

The men crouched behind their cars for cover, and all around the warehouse the sound of weapons being cocked filled the air.

Gun barrels twitched nervously from target to target. There were a lot of enemies inside the warehouse, and a lot of agitated fingers on triggers.

"Franco, we've found Baresi for you," shouted Stone.

Franco Cortesi stood at the back of his car with his gun pointed at Chang.

"Weally?" he replied. "So you're saying Mr. Scullen is Bawesi?"

"That's right."

"For the last time," roared Scullen, his voice booming across the empty warehouse, "I am not Baresi!"

"We were just about to bring your diamonds back, Franco," shouted Surpress, his gun still on Scullen. "We waited for these two to steal them, then we pounced."

"That's a lie!" shouted Fingers. "We weren't driving the van, we were told to come here by Baresi, and those two were going to kill us and keep the diamonds. They're working with Baresi."

"Shut your face, you sniveling little rat!" screamed Surpress.

Cortesi's eyes narrowed as he turned and pointed his gun at Chief Stone.

"How did you know?" Cortesi asked him.

"Know what?"

"Know that my diamonds would be stolen today? It was vewy intuitive of you."

The warehouse fell silent as Stone searched for an answer.

"I'll tell you how." Mickey Chang's soft voice was now raised in an angry yell.

Cortesi spun back toward the limousine. Mickey Chang was crouching beside his car, his small hands clutching a big gun, which he aimed across the hood toward Cortesi and the two policemen.

Chang's eyes and forehead were the only parts of his face visible above the metal.

"He knows because those two goons of yours have double-crossed us both!"

Cortesi turned his gun on Dumb and Dumber.

"They were only supposed to tell me; they must have told Baresi as well!"

"This is outwageous," screamed Franco angrily. "I'm suwwounded by twaitors and double-cwossers!"

"To be fair, Boss," Tweedle-Dumber wheedled, "we were only working with Mickey Chang; we had nothing to do with Baresi."

"Oh well, that's all wight, then," replied Cortesi. "I'll only kill you the once."

Tweedle-Dumb edged behind the car, beside Dumber.

"I'm going to kill evewybody!" Cortesi shrilled. He swiveled on the spot, his gun passing the face of every man in the warehouse.

"Did you tell anyone else?" Tweedle-Dumb whispered to his partner in crime.

"No," replied Dumber, "the only people we told were Mickey Chang and —"

The realization stopped the words on the brink of his tongue. Both men turned to each other.

"The Dubbles!"

"So if you two weren't driving the van," shouted Surpress excitedly, his gun flicking between Scullen and Fingers, "whoever smashed it through those doors must still be here!"

Fingers looked up to the door at the top of the steel stairs and remembered the loud crash. "Someone went up there."

Jake and Aidan lay on the roof and peered over the side of the building. At the end of the street two police cars blocked the road, their blue roof lights flashing in sequence.

"They've cordoned off the whole area, Jake," said Aidan. "They're on every corner. What are they waiting for?"

"The SWAT units," Jake replied. "They know whoever is in this warehouse has guns. They won't come near until they're locked and loaded."

Jake rolled onto his back and dialed a number on his phone.

"Jake, where are you?" Eddie answered.

"We're on the roof. Are you nearly finished?"

"Not yet. Give us five more minutes."

Jake put his phone back in his pocket.

"Are we good to go?" asked Aidan, picking himself up.

"Not yet." Jake grabbed his arm and pulled him back down. "Five more minutes."

"Five more minutes!" panicked Aidan. "We might not have that long before they realize we're up here. We might be dead."

"If we go before they say so, we will be dead. We'll never make it."

The two police cars at the end of the street reversed away from each other. Three long black armor-plated police vans rolled through the gap toward the front entrance of the warehouse.

"Here come the police now," exclaimed Jake as the rear van swerved across the road and stopped. Its back doors burst open and officers wearing helmets and Kevlar bulletproof vests sprung from inside, clutching machine guns.

The other two vans continued down the street; the first drove straight past the large front entrance to the warehouse but the second stopped straight across from it.

Officers poured out onto the street from inside them and took up their positions behind cars.

"This is the police," boomed a loudspeaker on top of the middle van. "The entire warehouse complex is surrounded by officers from the SWAT unit. There is no way of escape."

"Here we go," Jake said to Aidan. "It's all about to kick off."

Cortesi stood motionless behind his car, watching all the men around him point their guns at one another and panic.

"What a pwedicament we're all in!" he shouted to the others. "Evewybody comes looking for Fwanco's diamonds, but instead they find death or a long time in pwison. It seems Bawesi has set us all up."

Cortesi popped the bullet magazine from his gun and checked the ammunition inside it. With a short, sharp click the holder was back in the gun, and a bullet waited in its chamber.

"Nobody is taking my diamonds fwom me!"

Cortesi lifted his gun and shot at Mickey Chang's limousine. Its side windows shattered as the bullet passed through the car and hit the wall behind.

"I'm going to shoot you dead, Cortesi!" shouted Chang, pointing his gun over the hood of his car and firing. The bullets missed Cortesi but hit the side of his Jaguar, peppering holes in the door.

Instantly a barrage of gunfire erupted all around the warehouse as nervous men opened fire and shot at anyone they considered to be an enemy.

Scullen dived behind a car and curled into a ball on the ground.

Glass smashed as bullets ripped through the air and shattered windows in the warehouse walls. Men ran for cover as the rounds slammed into the walls behind them.

Chief Stone slumped in front of his car as a bullet glanced off a steel beam and tore through his thigh.

"Get up on the woof," yelled Cortesi to three of his men, "and kill whoever is up there! Kill Bawesi!"

Outside a few stray bullets made holes in the side of the police van.

"Return fire!" a voice commanded through a loudspeaker.

Armed officers took aim through windows and doors, and shot back at the men inside the warehouse.

"This is crazy!" screamed Fingers, crouching beside the front of a car; bullets smashed its headlights as he ducked for cover.

Jake looked through a crack in the door, down into the chaos below.

"We have to go, right now," he said to Aidan as he watched three men ascend the stairs toward them. "Right now!"

Jake picked Aidan up and almost dragged him to the edge of the roof.

"Get out, Eddie! We have to go now!" he shouted into his mobile. "We've got three men coming up to the roof."

"Three what?" Aidan asked in horror.

"Are you ready?" Jake was out of breath.

"I don't know," replied Aidan.

Jake grabbed his friend by the face and looked sternly at him.

"We have to do this, and we have to do it now. Are you with me?"

"Yes," said Aidan defiantly, nodding his head.

"Let's go!"

Jake and Aidan screamed as they sprinted across the top of the roof as fast as their legs could carry them. Jake dropped his coat down his arms and let it fall to the ground behind him.

Aidan threw his jacket down a ventilation shaft as he sprinted past.

THE ICE CREAM CON

Both of them were wearing sumo suits beneath their street clothes.

"Inflate now!" shouted Jake as they passed the metal door and ran toward the rear of the roof. Jake grabbed the toggle hanging from the front of his suit and pulled down hard. Instantly the suit began to inflate.

The door at the top of the stairs opened behind them. A long gun barrel appeared through the gap.

Jake looked over his shoulder and saw three men creep out onto the roof.

"Over there," one of them shouted, pointing toward Jake and Aidan.

The rubber of the two inflated suits squeaked loudly as Jake and Aidan tore along the roof to its edge.

"Get ready to jump!" yelled Aidan.

Bang!

A single gunshot screamed through the air. Jake felt something hit him on the side and his suit started to deflate.

"I'm hit, Aidan, I've been shot!" he shouted as his foot reached the edge and he jumped from the roof.

His legs kept running but all that was beneath his feet was thin air. He began to plummet down toward the street below, with Aidan tumbling through the air above him.

The cold wind flapped violently around them, stealing their breath as they fell, faster and faster and faster.

Police officers at the far end of the street watched, openmouthed, as two rotund figures dropped from the sky.

Jake held his breath and waited for the impact.

Harvey and Eddie watched from the side of the road as Jake and Aidan plunged straight into the truck's trailer.

Loud bursting sounds filled the air as they landed on a squashy bundle of inflated sumo suits, softening their fall until they came to rest on a pile of deflating rubber.

"Jake, are you OK?" Aidan scrambled through the suits toward him. "Where were you shot?"

"I think it was my side," replied Jake wearily. "Don't wait for me, Aidan. Get out of here now."

Aidan looked down at Jake and then turned him over.

"You're not shot!" he said, rolling him back. "There's no blood! The bullet went straight through your suit."

"I know," wheezed Jake, grinning, "but I'm loving the attention."

Aidan pushed Jake's face down among the suits.

"Hurry up, dudes!" Harvey banged on the rear door of the truck. "The police are going to come down here any minute."

At the end of the street, two police officers stood waving their arms at Harvey and Eddie, urging them to run toward them.

"Dudes, hurry up," Harvey spoke through his teeth as he smiled and waved back.

The trailer erupted with noise; it got louder and louder until suddenly the back doors burst open. Inflated sumo suits sailed through the air everywhere as Jake and Aidan jumped through them on ATVs . . . the same ones Eddie had helped Jake nick from the Numb Nuts.

The tires on both ATVs bounced on the road as Jake and Aidan skidded them around in front of Eddie and Harvey. Blown by the wind, sumo suits rolled up the street toward the police.

"Where's Sofia?" asked Jake as Eddie climbed onto the back of his four-wheeler.

"We don't know," he replied. "She disappeared. We think she freaked out and went home."

"Sofia doesn't get scared," said Jake, pulling back the throttle and speeding away from the scene of the crime.

Aidan zigzagged behind him with Harvey clinging on for dear life.

"Remember, head for the wasteland beside the east wall!" shouted Jake to Aidan. "There's a small patch of woods there that runs beside the railroad tracks. We'll make it through the woods, but the police won't."

The ATVs bounced over the pavement as Jake rounded the corner at the east wall and steered through some wasteland. Aidan chose a path over some particularly rocky terrain, forcing Harvey to grab him even tighter around the chest.

"Owww! Let go, Harvey. You've got my skin!" squeaked Aidan.

"Sorry, dude," replied Harvey, loosening his grip.

"That's all right, but when we get home I would like my nipples back. If that's OK with you."

Jake's phone started to vibrate inside his pocket. He pulled it out and saw Sofia's number on the screen.

"Where are you?" he answered.

Jake could hear a barrage of gunfire through the earpiece as Sofia screamed.

"Jake, I'm trapped in the warehouse!"

"You're what?" Jake skidded his ATV to a stop. "What are you doing in there?"

"My phone was in the glove compartment, I had to get it back!"

Jake heard Sofia scream as glass smashed all around her.

"I'm trapped beside the van!"

"Just stay still; don't move," Jake ordered. "I'm coming to get you."

Aidan pulled up beside Jake.

"What's going on?" he asked loudly. The noise of the gunfire from the warehouse could still be heard behind them.

"Eddie, get on behind Harvey," said Jake, slipping the phone back into his pocket.

"Where is she?" asked Eddie.

"She's inside the warehouse, trapped. Now get on Aidan's ATV."

"Hang on, Jake," said Aidan. "You can't go back in there — it's suicide, you'll get shot to pieces."

"Well, I can't leave her in there, can I?" Jake snapped. "She's only there because of me. I'm going back for her. Now, Eddie, get off!"

Eddie reluctantly climbed off Jake's four-wheeler and clambered onto Aidan's, behind Harvey.

"Just head for the woods, Aidan, and don't stop unless you're back in Lochrannoch or Harvey loses control of his bladder again."

"It only happened one time," Harvey mumbled under his breath.

"Good luck," Aidan replied.

"Go on, get out of here."

Aidan sped off across the wasteland toward the woods. Jake took a deep breath and turned his ATV around toward the warehouse.

The sound of gunfire surrounded the imposing brick building as the gun battle continued inside. At the far end of the warehouse he could see the two police cars that had moved aside to let the armed backup through. Their lights continued to flash as the fight for control raged on: police fighting gangsters, gangsters fighting gangsters.

Jake yanked back the throttle and the ATV's two front wheels lifted off the ground as the rear ones fought for grip amid a cloud of tire smoke.

Eventually the vehicle hurtled forward.

The wasteland blurred past as Jake gathered pace and headed straight for two wooden doors in the facing wall of the warehouse.

The engine whined as Jake opened the throttle as far as it would go.

The front tires of the bike hit the smooth blacktop on the road as Jake erupted from the wasteland and careered toward the wooden doors.

"Aaaaarrrggh!" he screamed as the machine slammed into the wooden doors and smashed them from their hinges. Pieces of timber framing landed on the back of the ATV as the heavy doors flipped inside, twirling across the floor before falling flat in the middle of the warehouse.

Jake revved his engine in the doorway and looked for Sofia.

The bullets continued to rip through glass and metal as up ahead the gun battle showed no signs of abating.

Men rolled around the floor firing shots at one another. Machine guns sprayed bullets over walls and cars as pandemonium descended.

Huddled beside the ice cream van near the back wall was Sofia. She cowered as bullets banged into the metal side.

Jake took a deep breath and sped across the warehouse toward the mayhem.

The growl of his engine echoed off the walls as the ATV gathered momentum and shot headlong into the line of fire.

Fingers squeezed triggers and bullets burst from chambers as all around him the madness continued. Empty shells landed on the ground; rounds of fresh ammunition sliced through the air.

Jake felt that time was slowing down. It was as if he were traveling in slow motion, watching and waiting. Waiting for the one bullet that would tear through his sumo suit and send him tumbling from the ATV.

"Jake!" screamed Sofia as he sped through the bedlam toward her.

Tweedle-Dumb felt a bullet graze his shoulder and threw himself inside his car, his legs still stuck out the door. Reaching up, he selected R on the stick shift and pushed the accelerator down with his hand. Smoke belched from the exhaust as the car careered backward, out of control, straight toward Sofia.

"Sofia, look out!" screamed Jake.

Jake pulled the throttle back as far as it would go and raced toward where Sofia crouched beside the van. The car gathered speed and hurtled toward her.

Jake stood on his seat, and as he reached her he yanked the handlebars sharply to the side. The bike flipped over, propelling Jake through the air. He hit Sofia hard and both of them tumbled across the concrete floor. Tweedle-Dumb's car smashed into the side of the van, missing them both by inches.

"You were nearly squashed, Sofia!" said Jake, rolling over beside her. Sofia sat up and looked at the crumpled heap of twisted metal and broken glass right where she had been.

"You saved me, Jake," she mumbled as she eyed the carnage.

"That's one you owe me!" Jake shouted as he pulled Sofia to her feet. "I'll remind you about it tomorrow, at the cash machine."

"Well, well, if it isn't Jake Dwake!"

Jake turned slowly to see Cortesi pointing a gun at his head.

"No!" shouted Jake. He closed his eyes and waited for the shot.

It didn't come. Jake heard a muffled thud and opened his eyes.

Cortesi lay spread-eagled on the ground. The enormous figure of John Joseph Scullen stood over him, rubbing his fist.

"You?" he said to Jake. "What are you doing in here? Get out; this is no place for a couple of kids."

Bullets flew up the wall behind him and Scullen dived down behind the van.

"You'll get yourself killed," said Scullen as he shuffled toward them. "Now get back on your motorbike and go."

"You saved my life." Jake stared wide-eyed back at him.

"It won't count for much if you get a bullet between the eyes now," replied Scullen. "Just get out of here."

"What about you?" asked Sofia.

"I'm going to try and leave here with the same number of holes in my body that I came in with."

"You'll get sent back to prison," said Jake. "You should never have trusted Cortesi seven years ago when you took the diamonds."

"I didn't," Scullen sighed as more bullets hit the side of the van. He seemed oblivious to the danger. "I didn't take the diamonds. I was set up. I did seven years for stealing diamonds I knew nothing about. So I said to myself, 'If you've done the time, you might as well go back and do the crime.' That's why I came back for the diamonds."

"Rubbish," said Jake curtly. "You're lying, your body language gives it away. I quite clearly saw your lips move. It's a schoolboy error."

Scullen seemed oblivious to Jake's sarcasm.

"You know what" — Scullen's voice trailed away — "I actually wish I was."

Jake looked at Scullen and in an instant could see what he'd missed that morning in his apartment; a man broken by years of wrongful imprisonment, a good man.

"Anyway, this is insanity," Scullen shouted, turning to Jake. "I can't get out, but you can; get your girlfriend on the motorbike and get out!"

"Yes, you can," replied Jake.

"I can what?"

Jake held out a set of keys. "These are the keys to the ice cream van. The diamonds should still be inside. There's a doorway I've busted open at the far side of the warehouse. At the end of the street there are only two cop cars, you'll make it through them."

"Where did you get these?" asked Scullen, trying to figure it out. "How do you know—"

"Do you want to play twenty questions?" Jake interrupted him. "Or do you want to get out?"

Scullen got to his feet and looked around the warehouse.

"I'll drive behind those cars." He pointed to his right. "Stay to the side of the van and I'll shield you."

Scullen raced around to the front of the van. Bullets tore through the windshield as he bent over and with unnatural ease flipped the ATV back onto its four wheels.

"Let's go!" shouted Jake to Sofia as he watched Scullen climb into the van's driver's seat and start up the engine. The two of them sprinted to the motorbike and jumped on.

"Hold tight," said Jake as he turned the key and the engine burst to life. Sofia put her arms around his waist and clasped her hands together.

The van sped away. Jake raced after it and pulled alongside as they roared down the back wall. Bullets riddled the side of the van as Scullen pressed harder on the accelerator.

"Stop the Mr. Freezee van!" screamed Mickey Chang, peering over the hood of his limousine. His normally immaculate suit was covered in dirt and oil, the result of rolling around a warehouse floor trying not to get shot. He fired at Scullen. "The diamonds are still inside!"

The bullets hit the back of the van as Scullen floored the pedal. Jake pulled in front and accelerated through the door, out into the daylight.

The side of the van scraped through the doorway as Scullen forced his way free in his unlikely, bullet-ridden escape vehicle.

Jake turned toward the wasteland and the woods just behind it, and Scullen steered toward the two police cars at the end of the street.

Jake skidded the ATV to a stop as he watched Scullen race at full speed toward the two cars. The officers dived for cover as he plowed the van through them. There was a loud smash as metal crunched metal and the two police cars were swatted to either side.

"He made it," said Jake, watching as the van headed for the main road and turned out of sight. A loud burst of chimes filled the air in the distance.

"Harvey won't be happy. There was a half pint of Tutti Frutti left in that van."

Sofia gripped Jake tighter around his waist.

"Are you OK?" He looked to her.

"I'm fine now." She smiled back at him.

"Good," said Jake. "Let's go home."

CHAPTER 28

Jake sat on the parking lot fence and allowed the sun to warm his face.

The projects were lively, as an unexpected spate of good weather had brought the residents out in droves. Children kicked soccer balls and rode bicycles around the grass in front of the buildings. Men washed their cars in between pulling up their jeans, as the sagging material almost always exposed too much of their backsides.

Jake laughed as he swung his legs between the fence slats.

There was an atmosphere around the projects that hadn't been there for a very long time. Apprehension was replaced by elation. Fear had been evicted by thrills. Despair was buried under hope.

It had been a little over three weeks since Cortesi and Chang had been arrested, along with most of the housing projects' criminal fraternity, in an abandoned warehouse in Glasgow.

The elusive Big Baresi had somehow managed to escape, so the gossips said anyway, and he was watching over Lochrannoch from a distance, ensuring that no other aspiring crime lord would see the projects as the place to set up home.

Across the parking lot a man opened his car door to clean the windows from inside. His car stereo blared out midway through a news report:

> *Police today said they were scaling down the investigation into the Fruit Market shootings in Glasgow a few weeks ago. They confirmed they had made a number of high-profile arrests at the scene of the shooting that left sixteen men with gunshot wounds, though miraculously there were no fatalities.*
>
> *Police spokesman Detective Inspector Lewis Telford said they would now be proceeding with the immediate prosecution of some of Glasgow's key underworld players. When asked whether the police would be continuing with the hunt for criminal kingpin the Big Baresi, Officer Telford said, "I'm not too sure, I'm quite new to this detective game, you see."*
>
> *In other news . . .*

The radio report disappeared as the man closed the door and locked his car.

Jake smiled.

"New to this game." He laughed to himself.

In his hands he held a white envelope with his name and address handwritten on the front. It was the first time he had ever received mail addressed to him that wasn't part of a magazine subscription or an attendance note from his school.

Jake rolled the letter between his fingers.

He didn't recognize the handwriting, so he knew exactly who it was from.

Eventually he tore open the top and lifted out the piece of paper from inside.

The handwriting was a bit untidy.

Dear Jake,

I hope this letter finds you both in good health.

It has taken me a long time to understand exactly what happened that day.

The truth is I'm still not sure I fully understand. I've gone over things a thousand times in my head, trying to work it all out, and just when I've ruled out the most ridiculous and far-fetched explanation in my mind, it keeps coming back to me, that it is the only possible rationalization.

You did it.

I still don't know how.
What I do know is that you saved my life, and
I saved yours.
I owe you, and you owe me.
Remember that, Jake. I will come back to it later.
It was only a few weeks ago that my life changed
forever, but it seems much longer.
That was when I first heard the name Baresi.
I wonder what it was that brought him to
Lochrannoch Estates. Maybe one day you
will tell me. . . .

Jake looked up from the letter as four large vans and a dump truck drove down the road toward him. They trundled past him as he sat on the fence, and rolled to a stop in the center of the courtyard. Jake watched for a while before turning back to his letter.

I still miss the old place; it treated me well over the
years. My life has changed now, and I have you to thank
for that.
I wanted to give something back to you, and back to
Lochrannoch, as a way of saying thanks, so I've arranged
for some work to be carried out that I hope will
benefit you all.
Just a small sign of my "good intentions."
You'll know what I mean when it arrives.

Jake turned back to the vans as men in overalls slid open the side doors and emptied tools onto the ground.

Kids ran past as a small crowd of residents gathered around the men, nosily trying to get a handle on what was happening.

Jake jumped down from the fence and walked over.

Two men lifted steel fencing panels and placed them into large concrete blocks all around the derelict community center in the middle of the projects.

On one of the panels another man secured a sign. It read:

Lochrannoch

**COMMUNITY AND PLAY CENTER
REBUILDING WORKS**

FUNDED BY GLASGOW CITY COUNCIL AND BARESI

The smaller type beneath the big bold lettering made Jake smile.

"Oh, there you are, Jake!" shouted his grandmother. In her hands she clutched two bags of groceries that she'd bought herself. "What is going on?"

"They're rebuilding the community center, Gran," he answered. "They've received some funding from the Big Baresi."

"There you go." She nodded. "And everyone thought he was just a bad man. Your tea will be ready in fifteen minutes." Jake watched as his grandmother disappeared into the growing crowd. "Excuse me."

Pharrp.

The crowd cleared a path more quickly than usual before dispersing altogether.

Jake shook his head and looked across the lot. Aidan, Sofia, Harvey, and Eddie waved to him as they walked toward the building site.

Jake waved back. The letter flapped as he raised his hand, returning his attention to his mail.

I hope you live a long, happy, and trouble-free life, Jake Drake.

With warmest wishes,

John Joseph Scullen

"What's that, dude?" asked Harvey, stopping in front of him. Jake was still nose deep in his letter.

"It's a letter," replied Jake.

"Who's it from?" Eddie continued. But Jake hardly noticed, he was too busy reading the last line on the page.

P.S. I've gone and gotten myself into a spot of bother. I really need the Big Baresi. Do you think he would help?

Jake looked up from the letter at his friends.

"What's going on?" asked Aidan.

Jake didn't reply, instead just raised his eyebrows in feigned innocence.

"No way," said Aidan wearily. "Not again."

"Oh yes, my good man," Jake replied. "Baresi is back!"

THE END